CW01645827

The

Eden Book

Society

MCMXCIII

First published in 2026 by The Eden Book Society, an imprint of Cinder House Publishing Limited.

Print ISBN 9781917792745
ePub ISBN 9781917792752
Kindle ISBN 9781917792769

Cover design by Luke Bird / lukebird.co.uk
and Michael Lacey / michael-lacey.co.uk
Typeset by Steve J Shaw / white-space.uk
Copyedited and proofread by Dan Coxon / dancoxon.com

Printed and bound in Great Britain by Clays Ltd, Elcograf S.p.A.
www.deadinkbooks.com

Supported using public funding by
ARTS COUNCIL ENGLAND

Funded by UK Government

MIX
Paper | Supporting responsible forestry
FSC® C018072

Frank Sloan is a professional writer, private investigator, and semi-professional concert pianist with degrees in organic chemistry, archeology, classical philosophy, and with a license to practice law in Indonesia. He dedicates his writing to all his former brothers in the Marine Corps, both those living and those who have already entered Valhalla. He fights the good fight in Kansas City, MO.

The Eden Book Society

The Eden Book Society was a publishing house which produced horror novelettes for a private list of subscribers from its inception in 1919 until 2006, presided over by the Eden family. Handed down through the generations, the history of the Eden Book Society is intertwined with that of the Eden family itself – shrouded in mystery and occult intrigue, with many dark rumours emanating from their ancestral home of Irkwell Manor.

Dead Ink secured the rights to the Eden archive – a century of unseen horror, written under pseudonyms by some of the greatest authors of their day – and is reissuing the books as archival research unearths them. This book belongs to the 1993 series: eight vintage horror novellas, never previously available to the public. Join us as we bring a century of unseen horror out into the light...

THE REDNEXORCIST

Frank Sloane

The
Eden Book
Society

Ex Libris

THE NIGHT EVERYTHING WENT TO SHIT

PROLOGUE

NOTHING GOOD EVER happens in a Motel Six after eleven o'clock at night, and what was happening in Room 107 wasn't about to change that fact. The hotel's night auditor had a congenital inability to detect trouble, but even he'd felt uneasy when he registered this couple. As he told the police later, 'He was too big and she was too little. That's always trouble in a couple.'

Now, Father Glenn knelt beside the bed, holding Betsy Morales' tiny hand between his two enormous paws while she had her nervous breakdown. Her chest snapped up and down as she spoke, her head shook side to side like windshield wipers, and so many fluids washed down her face that Father Glenn wasn't sure what was sweat or tears or snot anymore.

'It's that little house I bought from my auntie,' she said, voice clinging to sanity by its fingernails. 'Ever since I bought it, that spirit drives all my people away. None of my family still talks to me. I thought it was a bargain, but now I've got nothing and no one and I'm all alone. The only company I got is that ghost.'

Father Glenn squeezed her hand.

'You got me, Betsy,' he said.

He had a voice like a black velvet painting of Jesus and a face like Elvis circa 1962. He wore sideburns and kept his hair slick and combed straight back like the men Betsy grew up around, and his short-sleeved shirt showed heavily muscled arms and the tattoos that covered them: long strings of sentences snaking out from under his sleeves, marching down to his wrists, crawling over the backs of his hands like ants, circling up and down his knuckles and every single one of his thick fingers like they were covered in rings.

'The Bible says evil spirits aren't real, but I've seen this one. She's angry and she's coming for me and she won't stop no matter where I go,' Betsy said. 'It makes me think everything I know about the Bible is wrong.'

'There, there,' Father Glenn said.

Betsy didn't know what he meant by that.

'I need answers, Father,' she said. 'I need to know what happens when we die.'

For a moment Father Glenn looked like another, darker man, then his big smile lit up, glowing 10,000 watts, his dimples blinked into existence, and he said, 'Wonderful things.'

Betsy had hoped for slightly more detail.

'But...' she began, and Father Glenn looked into her eyes and transferred some of his calm presence into her.

'But is not a word in the Bible,' he said.

Betsy was pretty sure it was, but her clothes came from Walmart and her faith came from Greater Word Revival Church of God so she was used to taking what she was given and not complaining too much. Father Glenn pulled a red bandana out of his pocket and dried her face the way you'd wipe tears from a child. It was the first time Betsy could remember a man touching her gently.

'Try to pray,' he said, standing up.

He kissed her on top of her head and the smell of his cologne reminded her of her father, and the air conditioning rumbling in the back window of the room might have smelled like mildew but it was drying the sweat on her blouse and she was starting to feel like she could handle whatever came her way.

Father Glenn walked to the dresser and pulled something out of the pocket of his blue jeans and put it down next to the TV: a little wind up toy robot. Betsy started feeling nervous again. She didn't like things she didn't understand.

'Early warning system,' Father Glenn said. 'That little guy goes off, you bang on the wall and I'll come running.'

Betsy felt sweat prickle her scalp again.

'You're not staying?' she asked, hating the high-pitched whine in her voice.

'It's not appropriate for an unmarried man and woman to share a room,' Father Glenn said, and that made sense but it didn't do anything for her rising panic. 'Anything happens, you bang on that wall and I'll be here. You've got the eyes of God on you, Betsy.'

He took her room key and went out the door, leaving Betsy alone.

Betsy tried to pray, but she was too scared to close her eyes, and praying felt insincere with them open. The state of absolute panic she'd been in all day had scraped her hollow. She had no interest in watching the TV. The only thing she wanted to do was drink a Pepsi or eat something, but the doctor had told her that she shouldn't have any more sweets and the only liquids she should drink were clear, and that left water and Sprite and she didn't much care for either one of them.

Betsy decided the best way to demonstrate her enduring faith in a loving God was to stick to her normal routine so she went to the bathroom, turned on the overly bright light and brushed her teeth with water. When she'd run from her house that morning, the one thing she'd grabbed was her toothbrush because she'd always believed that wherever you laid your toothbrush, well, that was home.

Over the sound of her toothbrushing she thought she heard the door open in the other room, and she froze, toothbrush still in her mouth, water running, listening. She wrestled her fear down and made herself lean backwards out the door.

The room looked the same. The air conditioner rumbled away. The door stood closed. She couldn't remember if the closet door had been open or closed before, but she was pretty sure it had been closed like it was now, and she wasn't about to open it and look inside.

She finished brushing her teeth. Pastor Emil had gifted her an oversized I LOVE GRANDMA T-shirt from the donation box and she put it on and got into bed. She figured the way to show this spirit she was strong in her faith was to go to bed like normal. That would be a poke in the eye for the Dark One.

But try as she might, she couldn't fall asleep with the overhead light on. Like it or not, she had to turn it out. The thought of crossing the room in the dark made her heart squeeze painfully, so Betsy came up with a plan.

First, she clicked on her bedside lamp, then raced to the door, switched off the overhead light, and raced the darkness back to bed. She slid beneath the covers – safe! She scanned the room in the glow of her bedside lamp. Nothing. She decided any noise besides the rumbling A/C might be reassuring, so she picked up the remote and aimed it at the TV. It didn't work.

She pressed every button and nothing happened. She tossed it on top of the polyester bedspread in disgust. Maybe there was a Bible—

POP!

The light bulb in the bedside lamp exploded. The room went pitch black. Blobby ultraviolet afterimages floated behind her eyes, her heart punched her ribs, and that's when the little toy robot on the dresser lit up and began to walk. It made a grinding plastic noise that felt way too loud in the dark room, took three steps, then fell over on its side, little plastic legs paddling the air. They ground to a halt and there was silence again.

Betsy decided she would rather be a coward than a fool, so she raised her hand to knock on the wall and froze, hand over her head, armpit exposed, knuckle less than an inch from the paint, because she heard something in the bathroom.

A dull metallic rattle first, then a muffled *KLONK* as something landed on the bottom of the fibreglass tub. Then hollow noises, wet noises, dragging, scraping, splorking noises, the noises you'd get if you pushed ten pounds of steak through a three-inch pipe. Squishing, skworking, slurping, then silence.

SLAP.

She knew what that was: the sound of a foot hitting bathroom tile.

Then another one – *SLAP* – and with the sound of cracking knuckles she'd heard many times before, the spirit stood in the bathroom door. The spirit of her little dead cousin, Patricia.

She'd been pretty once, before Uncle Mark got hold of her, but even after that her mother probably could have recognised her okay. It was when he wedged her up under the house and the raccoons got at her that the real damage was done. The family and the police searched for three weeks before they found Auntie Luisa's dog, Pogo, chewing on a scrap of Cousin Patricia in the front yard, and they looked up under the house where Pogo liked to go, and found their girl, soft and rotten, raccoon-chewed, eyes wide open and spiders in her hair.

Now she stood in the bathroom door of room 107 in this Motel Six, broken neck cocking her head to one side, arms showing at least nine new elbows. Her waist-length black hair had been her best feature but now it hung over her face. She wore the same white graduation gown she'd had on for rehearsal when Uncle Mark stopped by.

Now she hated. Betsy could feel the hate coming off her like waves of cold air, so cold it shrink-wrapped her skin tight to her bones and made her hair brittle grass. She stared at the ghost of her little cousin, her white robe glowing in the dark, and Betsy prayed that Patricia would go away and leave her alone like she had never prayed for anything in her life. But she prayed with her eyes open because she was too scared to take them off this hate-filled thing even for a split second.

Someone cracked their knuckles, someone snapped a bundle of sticks, someone broke a bunch of pencils, and the spirit leaned to one side, flung out a leg, hunched its back over in a spasm, and dragged its back leg forward. Patricia stood two feet closer to Betsy. Then she did it again.

Betsy knocked on the wall. She banged. She pounded with both hands, weeping, pushing herself back, pressing herself as far away from her little dead cousin as possible, halfway up the wall, knocking, hammering, banging, pounding on that wall.

Nothing happened.

No Father Glenn racing to her rescue, no man of God throwing open the door and letting in divine light, no righteous warrior of the Lord unleashing the Holy Spirit. It was just Betsy in her room all alone with the rumbling air conditioner and her dead, hateful cousin, long black hair swaying from side to side as she advanced, and now she leaned over the foot of the bed, and now her white hands with their bundles of broken fingers gripped the bedspread, and Betsy felt the mattress take her weight.

It was on the bed with her. Blessed Jesus full of Love: it was on the bed with her.

Something dark blurred across the room, a shadow moving fast, and a fist smashed into the spirit's face with a meaty *THWAP*. It sagged to one side. She heard a man exhaling powerfully and heard two more blows, and the spirit of her little cousin fell off the bed and hit the floor with a *THUMP*, then He stood at the foot of her bed, triumphant.

'Gentle Word of my Loving Lord,' Father Glenn's loud, strong voice proclaimed. 'In your face!'

He threw a right cross that hammered the rising spirit and it slumped back to the ground. Betsy saw Father Glenn in his sleeveless T-shirt standing proudly in his faith, keeping his guard up, displaying the books of the Gospels tattooed down his arms, across the backs of his hands, and over his knuckles. The Word of the Lord that let him touch the forces of the supernatural.

'I am punching you on behalf of my Lord and Savior, Jesus Christ,' he proclaimed as he delivered two quick jabs to the rising spirit's face. 'I am beating your spooky ass with the power of his Holy Love.'

He moved forward, eating up the distance between them, delivering a devastating left hook to its head that sent its skull lolling in the other direction.

The spirit got shorter, shrinking, fading through the floor, disappearing straight down, Betsy assumed, on an elevator right back to Hell. Then something cold circled Father Glenn's ankles, and the ghost rose up out of the polyester carpet, clawing its way up his body with a surprisingly strong grip.

Father Glenn stumbled backwards and knocked the TV off the dresser.

'Shut the fuck up in there,' someone shouted from next door, pounding on the wall.

The ghost hauled its way up Father Glenn's torso until it crouched on his shoulders, gripping his skull between its hands, sharp with splintered bones, and it leaned into his face and did something disgustingly intimate to his left eye.

Father Glenn screamed and fell to his knees, sagging forward, slumping against the wood laminate dresser, drained of strength.

'Shut the fuck up or I'm calling the cops!' the man next door shouted, muffled, through the wall.

The ghost flowed off Father Glenn's limp body and turned towards Betsy again. This time the hate it felt for her was a blast of Arctic wind. This time its hate felt so cold its previous hate felt like love.

'Our Father, who art in Heaven, hallowed be thy name...' Betsy prayed through chattering teeth.

The spirit came for her.

'...give us this day our daily bread, and forgive us our trespasses, as we forgive...'

The spirit leaned over Betsy.

'...those who... those who... those who...'

The spirit fixed her with its one good eye and Betsy made the mistake of looking into it and she knew she was going to die. Then a baseball bat smashed into the ghost's head. Patricia fell forward, bounced off the mattress and landed on the floor. Father Glenn flexed his shoulders, adjusted the grip on his Louisville Slugger covered in the words of the Lord. He had spent weeks burning the Gospel of Luke into it with a woodburning kit he got from Kmart. He'd spent a month praying over it. He had fasted. He had sung hymns to it, and now it smote his enemies.

He wiped black slime from his eyes and brought his Blessed Baseball Bat down on the ghost's back as it tried to climb to its feet.

'The love and light of my Lord Jesus Christ compels you to eat shit!' Father Glenn proclaimed.

Then he tossed his Holy Baseball Bat onto the bed, picked up the spirit by one arm and one leg, leaned backwards, and lifted it into the air. He kept his grip tight as he whirled around in a circle, gathering momentum, leaning back further and further, fighting centrifugal force, until he let go and flung the ghost into the wall.

The banging from next door continued, but Father Glenn didn't let that stop him from taking care of the Lord's business. He picked up the squirming spirit, lifted it over his head, ignoring its broken fingers clawing at his wrists, and he brought its down on his knee in a classic Backbreaker.

He heard its twisted spine shatter. He stood up and dropped it to the floor like a sack of laundry and turned on the room lights. The spirit was already losing coherence, dissolving into a puddle of black slime.

Father Glenn kicked its disintegrating corporeal form once for good riddance.

'Begone, unclean spirit!' he said, then added for Betsy's benefit, 'Trouble this child of Christ no more.'

The spirit smoked slightly as it dissolved into slime. Father Glenn watched it to make sure there were no more surprises.

'I came in while you were brushing your teeth and hid in the closet,' he told Betsy over his shoulder. 'You've got to stay one step ahead of the forces of darkness if you're going to walk the path of righteousness.'

He flashed her a reassuring smile, but she didn't say anything, so he looked back. Betsy huddled against the wall at the head of the bed and she didn't look reassured. In fact, she looked more terrified than before. Her face looked grey and slick with cold sweat.

Her mouth opened and closed but no sound came out. Her eyes were locked on the steaming, liquid mess on the floor.

'You all right, sugar?' Father Glenn asked.

Betsy Morales screamed, rising in pitch like a kettle boiling over.

'I know,' Father Glenn reassured her. 'It's a lot to—'

Betsy Morales's scream rattled the walls, and hurt his ears, rising, rising.

'Okay, Betsy, calm down,' Father Glenn said. 'I took care of the—'

She kept screaming, so loud he couldn't believe one human being was making all that noise.

'Now, see,' he said, getting annoyed. 'Now you're just overreacting.'

Suddenly, Betsy stopped. She grabbed her left shoulder as if she'd pulled a muscle and keeled over on the bed. She didn't move. The only sound in the room was the air conditioner, rumbling away in the window.

'Betsy?' Father Glenn asked. 'Betsy? You resting?'

Her bulging, wide open eyes didn't look like she was resting.

He reached out and patted her face with one hand. It was like patting a cinderblock. He felt for a pulse: nothing. One of her dead hands clutched her left shoulder.

'Aw, hell,' Father Glenn said to himself, and the strength of the Lord drained from his body.

He really wished people would tell him if they had a weak heart before he engaged in spiritual combat on their behalf. It was sad when someone died, of course, but now he also wasn't going to get paid. He supposed he needed to call her pastor, that Reverend Emilio fellow who'd gotten in touch with him. After that it'd be best if he made himself scarce. He knew from experience that not only was it pointless to ask for someone to cover his fee, the family would probably press charges if he stuck around.

A blue light strobed across the drawn curtains and Father Glenn experienced a familiar sinking feeling. He made himself walk to the window on wooden legs and look through a crack in the rayon drapes. Two police cruisers were parked at angles outside his room, taking up a whole bunch of parking spaces. Typical cops. The police were already standing in the door of the room next door, talking to a half-naked man wrapped in a towel. From his angry gestures towards room 107, Father Glenn figured it was their wall-banger.

This wasn't good for anyone.

Moving fast, he grabbed his bat but left his wind-up robot. They weren't much good after one use anyways. He shut off the window air-conditioner unit, and grabbed it on either side just as someone started banging on the door behind him.

'Police,' they shouted. 'Open up.'

With the sound of old duct tape ripping, Father Glenn took the weight of the A/C onto himself and dropped it to the floor with a *BANG*. The knocking on the door got louder.

'Open up or we're coming in!'

Father Glenn felt a humid breeze blowing through the hole left by the air conditioner. He threw one leg through it.

Behind him, he heard an unholy loud *WHAM* and then the metallic *PING* of shattering discount hardware as the police kicked in the door and surged into the room. Father Glenn turned to them, half in and half out of the air conditioner hole. One of them pointed a bright yellow gun at him and his gut contracted as he shouted in a panic:

'No, no! Goddammit, don't tase me—'

They tased him.

16 YEARS AFTER EVERYTHING WENT TO SHIT

CHAPTER 1

THEY CALLED MORNING chow at 5.30 a.m. but he stayed back, sitting on his bunk, neatly dressed in his blues, tattooed hands folded, praying quietly to himself. He heard everyone come back from the mess hall, dropping into their cells, grabbing ass and making sass, until the guards called Movement and they all made their way to the Yard for morning rec. He stayed behind.

Even after their echoes died away he didn't let himself move, he didn't allow himself to look up, he didn't stand and wander to his cell door. He didn't want to appear too eager in case they took it away again. He kept his head down and prayed.

He thought they'd forgotten about him. He thought they'd made a mistake or changed their minds. His chest started to tighten but he willed himself not to move as his ears roamed up and down C Block, listening for a key in the door, a buzzed lock, footsteps coming down the linoleum.

Cold sweat broke out under his arms like a rash and then – finally, finally – he heard the big metal door at the end of the unit give its mechanical raspberry and grind open and purposeful footsteps made a beeline to his cell.

'Glenn Rambeaux,' the guard said. It sounded like Williams, but he kept his head bowed. 'Report to the Property Room with your State gear.'

Only then did Father Glenn let himself raise his head. It wasn't Williams, it was Salvio. So much for his ears.

He grabbed his box and followed Salvio down the empty unit. They crossed over to the admin office, where he filled out a bunch of paperwork and got handed a bunch of paperwork in return: his medical file, education certificates, everything he had to show for sixteen years in state prison. They took him to the visiting room where the clothes he'd tried on the day before were waiting. On the way, he had to tell three different COs his name and ID number.

He traded his skippies for a pair of plastic flip-flops, and his blues for a pair of grey sweatshorts and a long-sleeved T-shirt. He didn't know what the weather was like outside but he knew it was fall, so he wanted to split the difference. He wished they'd let him layer but you only got one piece of top clothing and one pair of pants on release.

They handed him his gate money (a twenty-dollar bill and a debit card with the $14.01 balance from his commissary account) and he fingered the twenty in amazement – it was the first cash he'd seen in over a decade. Money looked like it'd gotten slicker and more plastic since he went inside. Then they had him cool his heels. That was prison. You could hurry up and wait your entire life away.

He figured he'd been sitting in the waiting room about forty minutes when Officer Brown looked up from his paperwork and Hooptie Ali walked into the room. He was a big man who filled the door from side to side, stretching his blue uniform shirt past the point of believability. Father Glenn had never been too sure on Hooptie Ali's national origins but figured him for having roots somewhere in the Middle East or maybe Turkey, but heck, for all he knew he could be Hawaiian. They'd never gotten intimate about their hometowns.

Hooptie Ali stood in front of Father Glenn, towering over him like a national monument, and Father Glenn stood up so that it didn't feel quite so unequal. He came to Hooptie Ali's shoulders.

'You getting out today,' Hooptie Ali stated in a voice like Isaac Hayes wished he had.

'Yeah, man,' Father Glenn said. 'Looks like it.'

'Bet you think you think I owe you something after that little incident on Unit B and shit?' Hooptie Ali said, making intense eye contact. 'Bet you think because you saved my life, Hooptie Ali owes you shit for that shit.'

The two men held their eye contact, Father Glenn's brown eyes and Hooptie Ali's darker than brown eyes, pulling him in like black holes, infinitely inexpressive.

'Well,' Hooptie Ali said, 'you're right. That was some savage shit, and I still don't understand what kind of messed-up bullshit it was, but I would have been one dead son of the great state of Georgia if it hadn't been for you, so we organised a little surprise present. It's waiting outside. Now get the fuck out, get drunk, get laid, and don't come back.'

Grinning, they shook hands, and Hooptie Ali led Father Glenn to the red prison van that would take him to the real world. He was the only passenger. It was driven by Bug, a jittery inmate from Unit A who wore his thinning hair in a ponytail. He didn't talk much, but he looked happy to be participating in someone's release, even if it wasn't his.

They stopped at the gate and Father Glenn had to do another name and ID call and response with the CO on gatehouse duty, then they did a van sweep with a mirror on a stick and the big chain-link fence rolled to one side like the rock being rolled away from Jesus' tomb, and Bug drove Father Glenn out into the real world.

He'd seen the parking lot and turn-in before, but not as a free man, not from the other side of the wire, not when it represented a landscape he could walk into and just keep on walking, not when it was just the start of possibilities that could lead him as far as he could go. All those options made him dizzy.

Bug turned right, rolled the van fifty yards and stopped at the visitors' parking lot.

'End of the line,' he said.

Father Glenn realised he needed to open the door himself, and so in a state of euphoria, tinged with no small amount of panic, he half-stood, shuffled forward, reached out, and opened the first door he'd opened for himself in sixteen years.

He stepped down onto the cracked parking-lot asphalt and stood for a moment, under the real sun, breathing real air.

'Close the damn door,' Bug said, and Father Glenn experienced another first.

Bug rolled off, tyres crunching asphalt, and Father Glenn stood, alone and unsupervised, and wondered what he was going to do with himself now. They'd put him at the parking lot, not the bus stop, so he thought that was part of whatever surprise Hooptie and the others had planned for him. Had they bought him a car?

He scanned the lot, and that's when he saw her: a vision standing against a Honda Accord. Curly red hair. Pale skin. Freckles. Tall and with curves in all the right places, chesty enough to let you know she was a woman. It was the first civilian female he'd seen in a long, long time, and just the sight of her leaning against her imported automobile moved him profoundly. It played a note somewhere deep inside him that he had never expected to hear again.

'Hey,' she called, looking right at him, and her gentle Southern accent was cool water on the hot rocks of his soul.

'Well,' he called back, rusty at talking to a woman, trying to remember his old skills. 'Aren't you a vision?'

She stared at him, but she didn't scream for help or get back in her car and lock the doors so he figured it was okay to approach. He slapped across the parking lot in his flip-flops until he stood just three feet from an adult female, with no plexiglass barrier between them.

'I'm here to pick you up,' she said, and if she'd said, 'I'm here to suck your brains out and lay my eggs in your empty skull,' he could not have been more surprised.

Father Glenn looked around to make sure she couldn't possibly be addressing anyone else, then he realised that this was what Hooptie Ali and the other officers had done for him. In their gratitude for handling that business in Unit B, they'd made sure he wouldn't spend his first night out in the real world alone. The generosity of the human spirit moved him so profoundly he felt pressure in the corners of his eyes, and he might have cried if he wasn't also about to whoop with joy.

'You sure I ain't here to pick *you* up?' he asked, and felt a little thrill as his old skills came back to him. She looked confused and he smiled. 'I'm kidding, sugar. It's been a long time.'

'Whose fault is that?' she asked.

'I blame the great State of Georgia,' he said.

She pushed herself off the car, not looking entirely thrilled, but that was okay. Banter changed over time and he'd been out of the game. He'd get his groove back. Plus, she was bought and paid for, so he had some guaranteed runway to get himself back up to speed. She walked around the car and opened the driver's-side door, and he realised she meant for him to get in on the passenger side. He looked down at the cardboard box in his hands, containing all his paperwork, and he figured, *To hell with it.*

He flip-flopped over to a garbage can, dropped the box inside, then flip-flopped back to the Honda. She peered up at him from over the gear shift.

'You don't have any luggage?' she asked.

'Travel light, leave at first sight,' he smiled.

He could have sworn she rolled her eyes but he might've been wrong.

Father Glenn got in. It smelled so good he could hardly believe it. The air conditioner was going, the radio was on, nothing smelled like piss – it felt so painfully normal, like he'd never been away.

As they pulled out, he asked if they could turn off the radio and roll down the windows. He'd been cooped up inside listening to other people's noise for years. He wanted to enjoy a little silence. She did both. He loved the feel of wind in his hair. It'd been so long.

He ran his mind's eye over himself, taking an objective inventory. Even though he was older, he knew he'd kept himself tight, like Robert Mitchum. His hair had gone salt-and-pepper but it was still thick and he knew a lot of the younger ladies had daddy issues which worked to his benefit. His waistline was still hard. He still had good arms. His tattoos had barely faded, not like some of the blurry atrocities he'd seen out in the Yard.

He snuck a glance at her. She showed a little leg, but not too much, and she didn't have any tattoos. She was young too, and fresh looking, without the hardness you saw so often in women's eyes after they'd been in the game for a while, and he thanked Hooptie Ali for getting him a girl who was clearly high class. She rolled to a halt at a stop light.

'You'll stay with me tonight,' she said. 'Tomorrow we'll find you something.'

Man, this gal was full service. Well, he had saved Hooptie Ali's immortal soul from the Abyss. It made sense the man had paid for the deluxe treatment.

'Righteous,' Father Glenn said.

The sun warmed her copper hair and he could smell whatever shampoo she used. She had good, smooth, strong hands on the wheel, and, suddenly overwhelmed, he realised that he wanted some contact.

He leaned towards her.

'No hugs,' she said, changing her weight on the pedals as the light turned green.

'Or kissing on the mouth,' Father Glenn smiled, enjoying the give and take, settling back into his seat. 'The rules never change. I get it.'

'You know I'm Amber, right?' she asked.

He couldn't remember if she'd told him her name, and she was too young to have been someone he'd slept with before going in, but he knew women on the outside took issue with all kinds of things these days. He felt bad he'd gotten her back up, so he put his hand over hers on the gearshift. He couldn't believe how soft it was.

'I've always been partial to Ambers,' he said.

'Your daughter,' she added.

Suddenly those soft smooth knuckles felt like boiling Hellfire. He yanked his hand back so fast it hit him in the chin. He couldn't hold onto a single thought. They all took off and flew around inside his skull like a swarm of bats. He did his best to look out the window, gathering himself. She suddenly realised exactly what he'd been thinking, as plain as if she'd opened up the top of his head and peered inside.

'Jesus,' she said, the single blasphemous word dripping with contempt.

'It's not my fault,' he protested.

'Nothing's ever your fault,' she said, and her foot got heavier on the accelerator, pushing him back into the seat. 'Leaving us wasn't your fault, the divorce wasn't your fault, all the trauma you put us through: not your fault. Now, I pick you up from prison after all that and you hit on me like I'm one of your hoochie mamas, but no, it's never your fault.'

He needed to defend himself.

'You grew titties!' he said.

Surely she could see that.

'Oh, Jesus,' she said, and this time she definitely rolled her eyes.

'Last time I saw you, you were flat as a board,' he explained.

'I was six!'

'Exactly!' he said, glad she was seeing it his way. 'And you didn't grow little titties either.'

'Would you stop talking about my breasts?'

The only way out was through. She needed to understand his perspective. Anyone could make this mistake. He wasn't a pervert.

'You had work done on them?' he asked.

'I'm not even going to answer that,' she said, staring straight ahead.

'You—' he began.

'If it's about my breasts, I don't want to hear it,' she said.

'But—' he tried.

'No.'

They rode for a while in silence. Suddenly, Father Glenn had a terrible thought.

'Oh Lord,' he moaned. 'You ain't a stripper, are you?'

By the time they pulled up in front of her condo, Father Glenn's worst fears were confirmed.

'It's every father's nightmare,' he said, wiping his eyes with the heel of his hand.

'I'm an accessory model,' she said.

He didn't care what they were calling it now. She needed to understand there was more to life than the pole.

'I blame myself,' he said. 'I left you and your mama and now you're on the pole.'

'I am not on the pole,' she said.

'Your poor dead mother would spin in her grave,' he said, then turned to her, earnestly. 'Daddy's here now, and I promise you, baby, I'm going to fix everything.'

'Don't ever call a woman who's old enough to drive a car and pick your ass up from prison "baby",' she said. 'And Mom's not dead, she's missing. That is very important for you to understand.'

He knew a thing or two about grief. How it made you cling to your delusions.

'I know how hard it can be to accept Mama's gone,' he said. 'But she's sitting with Jesus right now, laughing and playing, with not a care or worry in the world.'

'Mom is not dead,' she repeated.

'Let's pray for her right now,' he said. 'We'll go up into your living room and kneel together and speak to Mama, and you'll feel a peace and understanding that you never believed possible.'

'No,' she said, clearly still in denial. 'You're going to go upstairs and sit in my apartment and wait for me to get home from work.'

He checked the clock on the dashboard and another knife pierced his heart.

'It's ten in the morning,' he wailed. 'That's when they put on the girls with low self-esteem.'

She closed her eyes and for a moment she did look exactly like her mother.

'I can't even talk to you,' she said, and now she sounded like her mother, too. 'Look, I will be back in five hours and I will tell you everything I know about Mom. And tonight, we're meeting someone who can help us find her.'

A lot of little girls became mistrustful towards men and developed abandonment issues when their fathers were incarcerated for long periods. He'd learned that in one of those mandatory workshops you had to take before they let you out. But she needed to understand he was here now and had her best interests at heart.

'Tonight,' he said, 'we are going to sit down and discuss at least getting you on an afternoon shift. The lunch crowd never tips.'

She ignored his offer and shoved a key at him.

'Here,' she said. 'It's 6B. There's food in the fridge.'

'You got any beer?' he asked, sensing an opportunity.

'Do not drink,' she said. 'Do not smoke. Do not do anything. Just sit there, in my house, with your hands in your lap, and try not to fuck anything up for five hours.'

He took the key and she seemed to have a sudden thought.

'Do you have any cash?'

She needed money? This got worse and worse.

'You're a beautiful young woman,' he said. 'I haven't seen you dance, but if you've got your mother's sense of rhythm, there's no need for you to pay for stage time.'

She pressed her lips together – which he wished she wouldn't do, because then she really looked like her mother – and held out her hand to him, palm up.

'Give,' she said. 'All your cash.'

'But darling—'

'I'm not your darling, I'm not a stripper, and my mom's not dead,' she said. 'I don't want you to have any options for the next five hours other than sitting on the sofa and staring at the wall. Give me your cash.'

He pulled the twenty out of the envelope. And the debit card. Sometimes it was better to go along with them for the sake of peace. She snatched it from him.

'Now go. Sit. Wait. Apartment 6B.'

She pulled out, her Honda spraying rocks.

She could have at least said 'thank you'.

Father Glenn rubbed the key between his fingers as he flip-flopped his way upstairs and down the second-floor balcony hanging out over the little strip of yard. It would've been nice to keep that money and go find more stylish threads at a Goodwill or a Salvation Army someplace, but he figured domestic tranquillity was worth any price. He put the key in the lock, turned it, and realised just how much he'd missed that crunchy metallic sound. It'd been sixteen years since he'd unlocked a door. The door to 6B swung open and its wood felt flimsy after all those metal doors in prison.

Inside, it was a standard one-bedroom apartment, but to him it looked like a palace. There was a leather sofa and some kind of glass-and-chrome coffee table in the middle of the room. There wasn't a dirty dish in the sink. They were all clean, stacked on the rack, drying, cups next to cups, plates next to plates. She'd have made a good cellmate. On the counter separating the kitchen from the living room sat a big fishbowl full of pennies and nickels and dimes. Televisions had gotten bigger since he went away, and one crouched on a table across from the sofa.

After living in a six-by-eight concrete shoebox for sixteen years, the apartment felt like Buckingham Palace, and he couldn't get over how nothing smelled like all-in-one sanitiser. He liked how the colours of the furniture matched the colours of the framed prints. She had probably learned that from her mother. She'd been a classy lady.

He'd gotten a letter about ten months ago when she'd died. He'd asked to attend the service, maybe even say a few words, but one of his arresting officers had taken his attempts to avoid incarceration personally and made certain comments during his testimony which meant they still classified him as a flight risk, so it was 'request denied', as usual.

He'd asked what had happened and been told she'd gone away on a business trip for the law firm that employed her, and one morning, for reasons Father Glenn couldn't understand, she'd woken up at five a.m. and gone jogging on a trail in a nearby park. Then she just disappeared.

The word was she was happy at work and about to get a promotion, and she didn't have nobody in her life who might want her dead, and her law firm did corporate work so it's not like some old client might have held a grudge, and she'd lived the life of a nun ever since Father Glenn divorced her all those years ago so all her old boyfriends were either happily married or currently incarcerated.

The authorities had looked for her for three solid months, until the story'd fallen off the front page of the paper and finally even disappeared from the 'Local News' section inside. Anything could've happened. She'd maybe gotten eaten by a bear or a feral pig, could've jumped into the lake to cool down after her swim and the cold water had given her a heart attack – she might even have run off to another town and changed her name in a fit of amnesia and right now was working the register at a Bi-Lo someplace, thinking she was a childless woman named MaryAnne. A lot of things could have happened. That's why he didn't jog.

He'd felt a certain melancholy. She'd been a comfort to him in hard times, so he put in a word to Jesus to be extra welcoming to the old gal, but for him once a relationship was over he didn't spend a whole lot of time looking in the rear-view mirror. He was all about the present and the future, not the past, and he liked to focus on where he was and where he was going, not where he'd been. It sure seemed like Amber was in denial, however. He hoped he wouldn't have to hear too much about it over the next few days while he got his feet under himself and figured out his next move.

He looked in the refrigerator but there was nothing in there but low-sodium water and half a loaf of pumpernickel bread. He tried to watch TV but there were three different remote controls on the glass coffee table and he didn't understand any of them. Five hours. He was a patient man, but did she really expect him to ignore his new-found freedom?

He looked out the front window. Amber's neighbourhood looked like it'd been full of working people once, but now there were a lot of plants in the windows and drawn curtains. Down on the street, he saw a handful of young people walking around, carrying iced coffees.

Across the street he saw an Evan Williams paint store, a Chinese takeout that wasn't open yet, and next to it a bar called The Lodge, with its door propped open by a cinderblock. Someone who looked exactly like the kind of person who'd go to a bar at ten a.m. went in the door. It yawned open, beckoning to him, singing to him its siren song. Father Glenn looked around the apartment and finally his gaze settled on that big fishbowl of change.

Five seconds later he was out the door.

CHAPTER 2

10.19 a.m.

'Finish this and hit the road,' the enormous, hairless bartender said, putting an ice-cold bottle of Bud down in front of Father Glenn.

'I do something wrong?' Father Glenn asked, ignoring this present beer in the interest of securing future ones.

'I'm not running a soup kitchen,' the bartender said, giving the stack of nickels totalling three dollars and fifty cents stacked up in front of Father Glenn a dirty look.

Father Glenn automatically went jailhouse Pavlov and opened his mouth to say 'Yes, sir,' then a feeling came over him more intoxicating than any beer, a feeling he hadn't felt in a long time, a feeling so new and dangerous that it made him lightheaded. He took a deep breath, picked up a nickel and spoke his mind.

'This here's legal tender. Same as paper. See what it says right there? "In God We Trust." And, son, I am a man of God. You are obligated to accept this in exchange for goods and services, and in return I'm going to sit here, enjoy my beer, and not make any trouble, because that is the American way.'

The bartender stared at Father Glenn for a long minute, then moved on down the bar, wiping the beer gutter. Father Glenn let the wonderful feeling of having stated his opinion bubble through his veins, like he'd just taken a sip of something better than beer. He picked up his ice-cold Bud and took his first sip and realised, nope, Budweiser still tasted better than feelings. He took another, deeper slug. And another. And goddamn, he'd forgotten what freedom tasted like. He didn't want to overdo it his first time out. He'd have one more for the road, then head back to the apartment and take a nap. Amber would never even know he'd left.

12.33 p.m.

'Shots! Shots! Shots! Shots!' the crowd chanted.

It was a small crowd, only about eleven lunchtime drinkers, but what they lacked in numbers they made up for in spirit. Father Glenn licked salt off the grimy side of the woman's neck, then threw back a shot of tequila and sucked the lime wedge out of her mouth. It got a little wet and sloppy after that.

'Shooooots!' the crowd cheered.

1.56 p.m.
Father Glenn stood on top of the bar. He raised the lighter to his lips and blew a fine spray of Jim Beam through it, sending a column of fire jetting across the dim room.

'Firebaaaaall!' the crowd cheered.

2.41 p.m.
'Over! The! Top! Over! The! Top! Over! The! Top!' the crowd chanted.

They had grown to about twenty-five people by now. They stood, surrounding a table where two college-aged girls, one in a baggy tie-dyed T-shirt, the other in white denim overalls with what may have been a shitstain on the seat, strained, hands locked, engaged in trial by arm wrestling.

No one showed any signs of leaving. Whatever awaited them in their offices and apartments was far less interesting than what was going on here.

'Over! The! Top! Over! The! Top! Over! The! Top!'

No one knew why they were chanting the name of a 1987 Sylvester Stallone movie. Father Glenn, who had started the chant, sat far from the crowd, beside a woman in a grey business suit who was drinking her lunch. While he admired Sylvester Stallone deeply for his singular vision and his drive, right now he was focused on a more immediate need. As much as he hated to admit it, he'd felt a powerful stirring when Amber had picked him up, but had understandably put it on hold after being informed of their blood relationship. It had returned, however, when this woman walked in the door of the bar.

'I kill ghosts for Jesus,' he told her. 'That's my earthly calling.'

'I think I'm an alcoholic,' she said, staring into the bottom of her Jack and Coke.

'I'm sorry,' Father Glenn said.

She drained her drink.

'I'm not,' she said.

3.17 p.m.

It was hard for the conga line to move through the packed bar, so it tipped over tables and threw chairs out of the way wherever it went.

3.55 p.m.

Father Glenn slow danced with shitstain overalls to 'Songbird' by Kenny G.

7.40 p.m.

Father Glenn sat with the circle of college kids who'd materialised around six-thirty because they had an ironic love of dive bars. He'd been surprised to hear he was in a 'dive bar'. Up until that moment,

Father Glenn had just assumed he'd been in a regular bar.

These kids were heaven sent. Businesswoman had been putting his drinks on her Diner's Club card, but now that she'd passed out the bartender refused to add anything more to her tab. Father Glenn needed to find another source of revenue to continue the flow of beer, so when these kids came in he immediately sat down at their table and wowed them with a series of magic tricks performed with empty glasses and drink coasters. They were on the hook. He just had to reel them in.

'Y'all know?' he said, lowering his voice so they all leaned in. An old preacher trick: the softer you talked, the harder they listened. 'I was the youngest child preacher in the south-eastern United States. They called me the Doogie Howser of the Bible Belt. And I've seen things that'd turn your curly hairs straight. Y'all want to know about the demonic forces behind the unchecked expansion of Walmart?'

He reached to one side without looking. Someone put an ice-cold beer in his hand. The Lord provides.

10.12 p.m.

Amber walked out of the 7-Eleven on the corner. She'd tried to describe her father to the clerk but couldn't come up with anything more precise than 'real

Southern' and 'slicked-back hair'. She'd wanted to say 'redneck' but she didn't think that was a word you were allowed to say anymore.

She'd already left three voicemails for Brian Belovic. The first one stated they were going to be running slightly behind, the second continued in that same vein, the third was abject grovelling, asking if they could reschedule.

One thing – she'd asked him to do one thing! – and he couldn't even do that. She'd never have gotten him involved if her mom hadn't asked, but about a year before she'd vanished, out of the clear blue sky, her mom had suddenly said that if anything ever happened to her, she needed to find her father.

Just hearing her mom say 'your father' made Amber's head rock back a little like she'd opened the fridge and smelled something rank.

'Why?' she'd asked.

'I'm only saying,' her mom had said. 'If anything happens, find your father and tell him.'

'Sure,' she'd said, and then she'd put her mom's request in the deepest, darkest closet in her mind where she stored everything having to do with her biological sperm donor, and firmly closed the door.

And locked it.

Twice.

She'd decided that her mom was just getting older and being weird about mortality, but when everyone else gave up searching for her, Amber finally poured a glass of wine, stared at her phone for a while, then opened the note her mom had given her that night. It had five names on it, each one a different alias for her sperm donor. It took a week of leaving messages until she found someone at the Georgia State Bureau of Prisons who was either nice enough or bored enough to call her back. The third name turned out to be the charm: Glenn Rambeaux.

She hadn't know what to expect when she'd pulled up in the prison parking lot, and she'd told herself that he'd been incarcerated for almost fifteen years so he wouldn't be at his best. She'd told herself the healthy thing to do was to let go of any pre-conceived notions, forget all past grudges, and accept him as he was. The important thing was to find her mom.

It had taken him all of five minutes to confirm every poor opinion she'd ever had of the man, and in less than twelve hours he'd lived up to every obscenity her mom had ever uttered against him. He'd thought she was a hooker and tried to feel her up. Calling him a pig was an insult to pigs.

She walked past a raging, out-of-control party spilling out of The Lodge. Great, as if everything wasn't bad enough already, now those assholes were going to keep her up all night. Amber went upstairs to her apartment, took a hot bath, and wished, for the third time that day, and the fifteenth time that week, and the sixty-seventh time that month, that she could talk to her mom.

2.34 a.m.

The bartender dropped another beer in front of Father Glenn.

'Three fifty,' he said, then moved off to help one of the thirty other people packed tight around the bar.

His businesswoman was unconscious again and Father Glenn had lost track of his fishbowl hours ago. He scanned the bar, looking for a way to pay for his beer, and once again the Lord showed him the way, leading his eyes to a drunk, passed out on the bar, face nuzzled into the crook of his arm, a pile of singles sitting by his elbow.

Father Glenn took a quick look around and then slowly reached over and slid the bills his way.

3.14 a.m.

The stall in the women's bathroom banged back and forth so hard the screws bolting it to the tile wall began to come loose. Inside the stall, the businesswoman and Father Glenn were having some of the most intense anal sex of their lives.

'I don't want to have some stinking baby,' she'd said.

'There's other—' he'd suggested.

'Up the butt,' she'd snarled. 'Or not at all.'

He'd chosen option A.

3.28 a.m.

'Shut up!' Amber yelled, leaning over the railing of the breezeway outside her apartment, wrapped in a blanket. The crowd outside The Lodge had gotten smaller but louder. 'Shut up! Shut up! Shut up!!!'

The crowd ignored her. She screamed at them until a neighbour yelled at her to shut up. Eventually she went back inside. This had been the worst twenty-four hours of her life.

6.11 a.m.

Passed-out bodies littered the bar. The businesswoman had disappeared. Shitstain overalls reclined in the arms of her arm-wrestling opponent, the two of them canoodling quietly in the corner. The bartender got ready to close up shop.

Father Glenn approached him, weaving from side to side, and slapped down a ten.

'It's been real,' he slurred. 'But I got to see a man about a dog. Two more for the road.'

'You're over the limit,' the bartender said. 'Cut your losses. Go home.'

Father Glenn squinted at him for a moment then pushed himself erect.

'Watch this,' he said, carefully.

He squeezed both earlobes with his fingers, hard, then pinched the skin between his thumb and his forefinger until he could feel his pulse tripping away in there. His swaying steadied. His eyes cleared. He held up one hand. It hovered in front of him, as still as a lake on a calm day.

'Reflexology,' he said in a smooth voice. 'Drunk as a skunk to sober as a judge in six seconds flat.'

A minute later, Father Glenn emerged, blinking, into the world. The bright early-morning sunlight made him wish he had some sunglasses. He drained his beer, tossed it into the gutter, then pulled another out of his pocket and slap-slapped his way across the street. He was actually amazed he'd gotten through the night and still had both flip-flops.

He went up the outside stairs of Amber's building and quietly slipped his key into the lock, then eased the door open, not wanting to wake her. He needed to keep her sweet while he figured out how to get a little cash in his pocket before he hit the road.

Amber sat on her sofa, fully dressed, arms folded, waiting for him. A mug of coffee steamed on the table in front of her.

'Hey, sweetheart,' Father Glenn said.

Her nose wrinkled as she smelled him from across the room.

'You're drunk and you smell like cheap perfume.'

Father Glenn raised a finger.

'Let she who liveth without sin not throweth the first stone. In a glass house.'

'Where'd you get that beer?' she asked.

Father Glenn looked down. She was right. He did have a beer.

'The Lord provides,' he said and chugged it gratefully.

'I asked you to do one thing,' Amber said. 'Sit here, wait for me, don't fuck anything up. Brian Belovic was supposed to meet us last night at six, but I had to cancel. And apologise. And now he's not taking my calls. Do you know how much work it took to get him to agree to meet with us in the first place?'

Father Glenn considered her words carefully.

'What's a Brian Belovic?' he asked.

'Do you remember anything I said to you yesterday?'

He thought about it.

'Parts?'

'Brian worked with Mom before she went missing,' Amber said.

Father Glenn looked blank.

'Mom went missing?' Amber prompted. 'Sheila Lieberman? Your ex?'

'Oh, honey,' he said. 'She's dead.'

'Why am I even talking to you?' she asked.

'I honestly do not know,' Father Glenn said. 'Why *are* you talking to me? Why'd you come pick me up in the first place?'

Amber was in the middle of taking a sip of coffee and had to summon all her willpower not to throw it at his head.

'I could have happily – happily – made it through the rest of my life without ever setting eyes on you again,' she said, her voice low and quiet, using every ounce of control she had within her. 'But a year and a half ago, Mom said, "If anything happens to me, find your father." And unfortunately something has happened to her and unfortunately you are my father. I figured, I hadn't seen you in nineteen years. You must have changed. But you're still the same irresponsible, lazy, selfish asshole you always were. You know what the difference is between then and now?'

'You grew titties?' he ventured.

'Back then I was too young to know how much of a piece of shit you were,' Amber said.

He hated seeing her get all worked up like this. He definitely remembered Sheila. They'd always had a good time together. And he remembered, kind of, a little redheaded squirt hanging around. She'd been too serious for a small child and she hadn't changed much since. He sat down next to her on the sofa.

'Sugar,' he said. 'Daddy's going to make everything better now, all right? The first thing we're going to do is find you a job where you don't have to shake your moneymaker for strangers at eleven o'clock in the morning, and—'

'I am not a stripper!' she shouted, standing, almost spilling her coffee. 'I am an accessory model. I spent yesterday holding handbags at different angles for a commercial shoot! Stop projecting your creepy obsession with sex workers onto me!'

She stood, shaking with rage like one of those little Mexican dogs that got cold all the time. He decided to move on gracefully. She was clearly not in a reasonable mood.

'Amber,' he said. 'If meeting this Brian Belovic is so all-fired important to you, why don't you give him a call right now, tell him I got over-served, but I'm ready now. See if he'll meet us at Denny's? I'm craving a Grand Slam.'

'He worked with Mom,' Amber snapped. 'He's not the kind of guy who goes to Denny's.'

'Everyone loves Denny's,' Father Glenn said.

'I don't.'

'Well, that explains a lot.'

He saw her portable handset on the coffee table and picked it up.

'What's his number?' he asked. 'I'll call and see if he'll change his mind about Denny's.'

Amber snatched the phone out of his hand.

'I'll call,' she said, and then realised she had to follow through. She'd dialled Brian Belovic's number so many times last night that she knew it by heart. To her surprise, he answered on the second ring. Father Glenn sat on the sofa, eyes closed, listening.

'Brian? Hi,' she said. 'Amber Lieberman. I am... I know, I am so sorry... I know... I know... you *are* a busy man, but my dad showed back up and I was wondering if you still had time to meet real quick... Oh? Oh! Great. No, really, that's great. Um, how about...'

She drew a blank, completely unable to think of a single place they could meet.

From the sofa, Father Glenn said, 'Denny's.'

'...Denny's?' Amber echoed because it was the only name she could pull out of her brain. 'Oh? Okay! Thirty minutes.'

She hung up.

'Apparently,' Amber said, 'he loves Denny's.'

Neither of them spoke on the drive. Amber pointedly rolled down her window because a thick stink of beer fumes and White Diamonds by Elizabeth Taylor radiated from her father. He leaned against the headrest with his eyes closed for most of the ride.

Amber would be damned if she was going to speak to him first, or cut him any slack, or make things the slightest bit easier. He'd be the next one to speak, and if anything but an apology came out of his mouth she was going to punch him in the face.

They pulled into the parking lot, still not talking, and headed inside. Denny's was crowded.

'No tables,' Father Glenn said. 'We'll have to sit at the counter.'

He headed towards it.

'You don't even know what Brian looks like,' she said, annoyed.

He stopped.

'Who?'

'Brian Belovic,' she said, scanning the tables.

'Is that your boyfriend?' Father Glenn asked.

It took a minute for the meaning of his words to sink in. Then it took Amber a minute to trust herself enough to speak. When she finally did, her voice was so clipped that every word was its own sentence.

'Have. You. Listened. To anything. I've said?' she asked. 'He worked. With Mom. He's meeting us. Here. I just called him. You were there.'

Father Glenn recovered fast.

'I'm testing you,' he said.

'Yes,' Amber agreed. 'You are.'

She turned away from him in disgust and the first person she saw, sitting in a booth by the window, was a tan man with slicked-back hair wearing a double-breasted grey suit and a red power tie. Someone dressed that nicely this early in the morning had to be someone who'd worked with her mom.

'Come on,' she said, picking her way across the crowded restaurant.

Father Glenn cast a yearning look over his shoulder at the counter, then followed. He always preferred the counter. You got to have a rapport with the waitresses. But he needed to make Amber happy right now. She was in a mood.

Brian stood up as he saw them approaching. He wore sunglasses indoors and a suit that Father Glenn thought made him look like an asshole.

'Brian,' Amber apologised, in a much softer voice than she used to speak to her father. 'I'm so sorry we're late.'

'Amber,' Brian said, taking her hand. 'Looking lovely. Is this Dad?'

His expression showed a micro-flicker of disgust and his smile got tight as he held out his hand to Father Glenn.

'I knew Sheila for nine years, and in all that time I never heard her say a single good thing about you,' he said.

Then Father Glenn took his hand, and Brian Belovic burst into flames.

CHAPTER 3

ONE SECOND, BRIAN Belovic was the kind of asshole who wore sunglasses indoors; the next, he was a human torch. Every pore in his body erupted like a tiny volcano, spitting fire. His suit melted off his shoulders, hung from his arms in charred tatters, then unravelled to the floor. His pants evaporated on fast forward and his belt fell down around his ankles, still in a loop. His hand spasmed around Father Glenn's and locked tight.

A million razor-sharp claws dug into Father Glenn's right hand, searing it like a steak. He pulled away from this burning, exploding pillar of flame, trying to get his body as far away as possible, but he couldn't break Brian Belovic's grip. The heat from his burning body singed the insides of Father Glenn's nostrils and crisped his nose hair.

Brian Belovic opened his mouth and screamed for a single split second before his larynx boiled shut and one-thousand-degree flames melted the flesh from his chin and split the roof of his mouth. Flames shot from the top of his head and licked the white acoustic tile ceiling.

It happened fast. By the time customers looked up from their conversations and their Moons Over My Hammys, the blast wave of superheated air from Brian Belovic was halfway across the crowded dining room and travelling fast. Diners watched this Old Testament apparition in frozen awe: a pillar of fire. No one could make their vocal cords work.

Something inside Brian Belovic's melting, bubbling brain fired a confused cluster of commands that sent him running towards the hostess station. He didn't see the party of three sitting there and he slammed into their table, knocking it to one side, setting the dad's hair on fire. That's when people started screaming.

Brian Belovic's eardrums had melted so he didn't hear. His burning body just ran right for the hostess station, slamming into tables, sending Mile High Omlettes and cups of coffee crashing to the floor, crushing packets of non-dairy creamer and slipping on blueberry pancakes in his panic.

Diners were up now, forming a blob that shrank from him everywhere he ran. He smashed into a busboy, who dropped his tray, adding to the chaos. He reeled towards the booths and people crawled over the dividers, dragging their crying children behind them. He stumbled into tables, sending them skidding into men trying to keep their women behind them. He knocked over high chairs, sending them crashing into the manager.

Promotional mobiles hanging from the ceiling went up in flames, dropping scraps of burning cardboard onto the screaming crowd. People made for the door, but then Brian Belovic stumbled towards it and they shrank back, pressing themselves into the far end of the dining room.

Everywhere he went, Brian Belovic dragged Father Glenn along behind him, whipping him through the wreckage like a tail, their hands clamped together in a blazing handshake. The flames scorched Father Glenn's forearm but they melted Brian Belovic's ligaments and tendons and, for one brief moment, he staggered to a stop, swaying uncertainly; and in that instant, Father Glenn braced his feet and brought Brian's wrist down on the back of a chair, hard and sharp. Through the scorched palm of his right hand, he felt something in Brian's arm break. Then he did it again, and again. He grabbed a knife from someone's steak and eggs and hacked off the strip of charred red-and-black muscle still connecting them, then Father Glenn pulled free.

The right side of his body finally felt cool. He spotted Amber crying – face wet, hands pressed to her mouth – at the front of the crowd, and he charged towards her. The two men beside Amber screamed and jerked away instinctively, pulling their children with them, but Father Glenn grabbed Amber by the arm and hauled her out the front door.

Outside, the sun seared his burned right arm and the right side of his face, but the cooler air felt good. He sucked smoke-free air into his lungs. Thank the Lord it didn't smell like bacon out here. Amber started to drag ass behind him, pulling them to a stop.

'Gimme your keys,' Father Glenn said, not giving her a break, walking fast for her car, dragging her along behind.

'We can't...' she began, looking back at the Denny's.

A waitress crashed through the door, pointing at them, screaming something that might have been words. Father Glenn saw a few pedestrians stop, looking from the waitress to them.

'We can,' he said.

Her car was just up ahead.

'The police...' Amber said, and pulled backwards, digging in her heels.

Father Glenn turned.

'I'm an ex-con stuck to a chopped-off hand,' he snapped, raising his right hand. 'Keys.'

The charred, semi-skeletal claw of Brian Belovic's hand was locked around his reddened fingers. For a second, Amber looked like she was going to throw up, but she reached into her purse and pulled out her keys. Father Glenn snatched them.

He slammed into the driver's seat and she got in. Then he used his left hand to awkwardly reach around the steering column and twist the ignition. He dropped the Honda into reverse, backed out, then shifted into drive one-handed and got them the hell out of there.

He held out his right hand to his daughter.

'Grab it by the base and pull,' he said.

The hand squirmed, like deep-fried snakes trying to crush his fingers. Its exposed tendons writhed like eager worms. A man with a sheltered-looking two-year-old in his arms goggled at them through the windshield. Then he started to shout something and Father Glenn realised they didn't have time to stick around.

He hit the gas and they slammed out of the parking lot and onto the road, pulling into traffic, which was fortunately moving. Father Glenn felt his back unclench with every block they put between themselves and the Denny's, but he was only half paying attention to the road, the other half of his attention on the severed hand still locked around his, trying to crush it.

He shook his hand hard. The moving fingers were really starting to freak him out. He shot Amber a look. She had to see the importance here. She'd turned white.

'I'm not touching that!' she gabbled, pressing herself against the passenger-side door.

'You don't have a choice!' he shouted back.

She just stared at the hand in horror. Didn't she see this was worse for him? Up ahead was a long straight stretch of road passing a bunch of big retail stores. It looked like green lights all the way to the highway, the on ramp shimmering in the early morning heat.

'Hold the wheel,' he told Amber, then let go of it so she didn't have a choice.

Automatically, she grabbed it and Father Glenn began breaking Brian Belovic's fingers one by one, like someone snapping pencils.

'We have to go to the police,' Amber said, talking loud enough to be heard over the sound of breaking bones, trying hard to hold onto some kind of reality. 'I mean, we didn't do anything wrong, right? It's just... it's just like he had an allergic reaction... I've read that some synthetic fabrics react with certain deodorants... maybe it was his Palm Pilot?'

Father Glenn changed tactics and tore Belovic's thumb off, rolled down his window, and flung the wriggling thumb out of the car. He followed it with the rest of the hand. Through the rear-view mirror, he saw it bounce three times then go under the tyres of a truck.

He grabbed the wheel and lifted Amber's hand away by her wrist. His entire palm felt gritty and greasy with Belovic soot. Amber yanked her hand back and clutched it to her chest. Father Glenn put on his right-turn signal and pulled into the parking lot of a Piggly Wiggly.

He found a space at the very edge of the lot. This early in the morning there weren't many cars, and most of them were clustered closer to the doors. He pulled on the emergency brake and they sat there for a moment. Then he turned off the ignition with his burned hand. Man, it hurt.

'You got any ointment?' he asked.

Grateful to be doing something normal, Amber opened her glove compartment and pulled out a plastic container of Wet Naps. Father Glenn used a fistful to scrape the warm human remains off his right hand. It was red and tender to the touch, especially on the palm and finger pads, but there weren't any bad blisters and he'd managed to keep his fingernails. It could be worse.

'You got forty dollars?' he asked, scanning the parking lot, not wanting to make eye contact.

She didn't respond so he reached over, pulled her wallet out of her purse, plucked out two twenties and stuffed them in his pocket.

'See you later,' he said, and got out of the car.

He was gone. Amber sat in stunned silence, completely motionless for a moment, then threw her door open and ran after him across the parking lot. She caught up to him just before he reached the sidewalk.

'Wait!' she said. 'You can't leave. Where are you going?'

'Miami,' he said, not slowing down. 'I'll find an old lady who needs someone to clean her pool and trim her hedges, maybe expect me to throw her a bone on federal holidays. If she'll let me stay in her guest house for free I'd consider it a fair trade. You take care now.'

He picked up his pace. Amber grabbed his shoulder and pulled him to a stop.

'What about Mom?' she asked. 'What about Brian Belovic?'

He kept his eyes over her shoulder, focused on Piggly Wiggly's eager, porcine logo.

'Your mother and I are divorced,' he said. 'And Brian what's-his-name is dead.'

Then he started walking away again.

Amber couldn't find the words to rebut his argument, so it just came out in an anguished cry.

'You can't leave me again!'

Father Glenn stopped, his back to her, shoulders hunched. He took a deep breath that sounded a little shaky to his ears, then he turned his expression back into stone and turned around to face his daughter.

'Let me give you a little advice,' he said. 'Mama's gone. She ain't ever coming back. I know you think she's still out there somewhere, but even if she is, you're better off leaving this alone. You don't need to ever see me ever again. Go find a man who'll put some babies in your belly and be happy. Send me pictures at Christmas. I won't cross state lines so you don't have to worry about me showing up to visit, but I'd like to see my grandchildren every now and then. Just in case I run into one of them in a bar down the road. But stop looking for your mama. Stay away from the place she worked and the people she worked with.'

'You can't ditch me,' she said, breathing hard from her chest. "Again."

He got the impression she wasn't listening, so he turned up the volume on 'cold' and tried again.

'Sure I can,' he said. 'First time was for practice, this time's for keeps.'

He turned and started for the waist-high cinderblock wall between the parking lot and the sidewalk. If he could just make it that far, if he could just put that between them, he'd be free. Then he'd hitch a ride, or charm someone, or, worst-case scenario, catch a Greyhound. All he had to do was reach the wall.

'You owe me!' she said, following him.

'What're you?' he asked, not breaking his stride. 'A bank?'

'You really want to run away like a coward?' she asked.

He decided to change tactics. Maybe if she knew how dangerous this was, she'd take what he was saying seriously. He took a deep breath and turned.

'Leaving you and your mama was the—'

Neither of them saw the TransAm. It knocked Amber's legs out from under her, and sent her rolling up its hood, over its low sloping windshield, and she would've gone straight over its roof but she went spinning, taking out the side-view mirror with one hip, then landed on her feet. The momentum sent her staggering around in a big circle, feet slapping to keep up with her body, then she went into a deep knee bend and fell, arms and legs useless. Even from this far away Father Glenn winced as he heard her head hit the asphalt with the sound of a coconut.

Amber opened her eyes. The light hurt. Gravity felt wrong. A crowd of people looked down at her, peering at her from a ring way up in the sky. She realised gravity felt wrong because she was lying on the ground. The ground was very hard against her back.

'Can you feel your toes?' one of the faces asked down a long cardboard tube.

Amber wiggled her toes. They hurt. She opened her mouth and made a sound.

'Anything broken?' the voice asked and she recognised the face. He was that guy. Her dad.

She let her mind travel through her body and sensed that it was basically okay. She sat up. Her head gave a sick lurch and everything took a slow ride on the merry-go-round for one full circle, then it stopped, steadied, and her head stayed on the end of her neck.

'No,' she said, staring down at the asphalt glittering with mica between her legs. 'Not broken.'

'Okay, then,' her dad said. 'I guess I'll be moseying along.'

He walked away from the little knot of people gathered around her. There were a lot of them. She wondered why they weren't saying anything. Her asshole dad flip-flopped away from her, rubber soles grinding the asphalt, the long right sleeve of his grey T-shirt scorched brown. Coward.

'I'm okay,' she said, cutting off any possible commentary from the people around her. 'But can someone take me to the hospital?'

No one said anything, and she looked around, trying to find the most sympathetic face.

'You should watch where you're walking,' someone said.

It came from a guy with a sunburned forehead who was failing to grow a moustache on his upper lip. Next to him stood a girl with a scrunched-up little monkey face. The other people around them slowly came into focus.

They were blistered, they had road rash on their faces, one of them didn't even have a face, just two round eyeballs staring out of what looked like a pizza with no cheese. Their clothes were torn and bloodied and charred and hung in rags. A little girl with no lips sucked a charred thumb in her skeleton grin, one eye glued to Amber, the other eye weeping down her cheek, suspended by its optic nerve.

Amber screamed. It was high and thin and hysterical and it didn't travel very far, but Father Glenn heard. He checked over his shoulder and saw Amber standing, lurching around the parking lot in a tight circle, flailing and cringing while the poorly-moustachioed teenager and his monkey-faced girlfriend watched.

'Get away!' she shouted at no one, facing away from Failed Moustache and Monkey Face. 'Get away from me!'

Father Glenn's feet slowed. He had a bad feeling about this. He stopped, then trudged back to Amber and grabbed her arm.

'No!' she shouted in the general direction of a Subaru minivan. 'No! Get away!'

'Hey,' Father Glenn said, pulling her around, snapping his fingers in her face, trying to get her attention. 'Hey!'

It didn't work. She looked around wildly at everything but him. He grabbed her chin.

'Who are all these people?' she asked, eyes bugging out of her skull.

Father Glenn had a sinking feeling.

'How many people can you see here right now?' he asked.

'I don't know!' she yelled. 'Fifteen? A hundred?'

Hellfire, Father Glenn thought. *This is exactly what I* don't *need.*

'Is she high?' Monkey Face asked.

Father Glenn took Amber by both shoulders and shook her. Hard.

'Ignore 'em,' he said, and shook her again. She finally focused on him and her lips started to form a word. He began dragging her in the direction of her Honda. 'Ignore them. They're dead.'

'What?' Amber asked, rooting herself to the ground.

'What!' Failed Moustache said, laughing like a hyena.

'Come on,' Father Glenn said, trying to drag Amber along with him.

She wouldn't move.

'What are you talking about!?!' she screamed.

'She came out of nowhere,' Monkey Face said. 'She, like, threw herself under our car. My cousin's a cop.'

The little girl sucking her thumb tried to take one of Amber's hands. Her skin was so cold that touching it burned. Amber yanked her hand away and pressed it to her chest.

'No!' she shouted.

Father Glenn tried to drag her towards the Honda again, this time using both hands.

'I know,' he said. 'I know, they look like a bunch of assholes.'

'You can't act like this in a Piggly Wiggly parking lot,' Monkey Face said, frustrated that no one was paying attention to her.

Amber tore herself out of Father Glenn's grip and backed away, trying to keep her eyes on all of them at the same time: the pizza-faced man, the little girl with no lips, her dad. Her butt bumped into something and she whirled and screamed, confronting the front bumper of a black Ford Taurus with tinted windows.

'Come on,' Father Glenn said, trying to take her wrist again.

'No!' she shouted, batting his hands away.

'Hey, Lady?' Failed Moustache called, thinking this was the most fun he'd had all morning. 'You want me to call the police on this guy?'

Father Glenn turned.

'Hey, Dickface?' he said. 'You want me to beat your ass into the ground?'

He looked scarier than he did a few seconds before.

'Are you going to let him talk to you that way?' Monkey Face asked, goading her man on. What made him look bad made her look worse because she was with him. When she saw that he wasn't going to do anything, she turned on the hillbilly dude who was trying to hold the screaming girl by both shoulders. 'Fuck you!' she yelled.

They didn't seem to care. Father Glenn leaned down into Amber's face.

'Look at me, sugarbun,' he said. 'Look at Pawpaw.'

She kept looking everywhere but at him, eyes darting over his shoulders, resting on something, then shooting back to the other side.

'What are they?' she asked. 'Where'd they come from? What do they want?'

'Lots of people die in parking lots,' Father Glenn said. 'Now listen, hold still, I'm going to get something from the car. It'll help you.'

Two minutes later they pulled out of the parking lot in Amber's Honda. Father Glenn put on his turn signal. Amber wore her gym bag over her head. She moaned, unable to talk or articulate a single coherent thought, just moaning because if she didn't let the pressure out somehow her skull was going to explode. Her moaning sounded muffled and hollow inside the gym bag.

'That noise is disconcerting, sweetheart,' Father Glenn said, pulling into traffic.

Amber moaned louder.

'You got any tranquilisers back home?' Father Glenn asked. 'Marijuana? Tequila?'

Inside the gym bag, Amber shook her head.

'All right,' Father Glenn said, pressing down on the accelerator and sailing through a yellow light. 'We're going to have to make some stops.'

CHAPTER 4

HE EASED AMBER gently down onto her couch, gym bag still over her head. She'd stopped moaning and lapsed into a numb compliance. He actually found that even more unnerving.

She sat stiffly in front of him, shoulders square, gym bag motionless, hands on her knees, and Father Glenn felt something approximating a paternal feeling twitch deep inside as he reached out and grasped the corner of the bag.

'I'm going to take it off on three,' he said, soothingly. 'One...'

He yanked it off. Amber screamed, then stopped.

There were no ghosts. She checked either side and behind her. Nothing. A tiny bit of tension went out of her shoulders, then she threw herself forward and looked under her couch. Nothing. She sat back up, pale and washed out, eyes still glazed with fear.

Father Glenn folded her fingers around a glass pipe and guided it to her lips. He brought out a lighter and started heating up the bowl.

'I want you to take a little bit of this,' he said, in his most fatherly voice.

'What is it?' she asked around the stem.

'Heroin,' he said.

She threw it. The glass pipe hit the coffee table and cracked in half.

'Fuck you!' she shouted.

'It takes the edge off,' he said.

'You're trying to give me heroin?' she asked, outraged.

'All right, all right, calm down.' He patted the air between them with one hand and reached behind him with the other. 'How's this?' he asked, twisting the cap off a mini-bottle of Popov.

She looked at him through slitted eyes, then grabbed it and slammed the entire thing, throat working. Some of the tension drained from her shoulders. He twisted the cap on a second bottle. She didn't even give him the stink eye this time, just snatched it out of his hand and put it away. And the third.

'Who's a thirsty girl?' he asked. 'One more...'

She took the fourth in two gulps, then dropped the tiny plastic bottle onto the sofa beside her.

'I'm drunk,' she declared, and let herself fall backwards against the sofa.

'Good start,' Father Glenn said. 'Now, I want you to look at something for me.'

He pushed himself to his feet, knees popping, and threw open the front door.

'See anything?' Father Glenn asked.

Standing in the door stood a man in a pair of denim overalls with no shirt. The top half of his head had been sheared away and pink porridge dribbled down his face. Amber stared at him, stricken, then she leaned over and threw up in her gym bag.

'Hypothesis proved,' Father Glenn declared, satisfied.

The ghost tried to step into the apartment but Father Glenn stopped it with one tattooed hand on its chest. He said a quick prayer, kissed his right fist, and punched it in the chin. It wobbled for a second, spilling skull porridge everywhere, then he gave it a helpful shove and it flipped backwards over the breezeway railing. As he closed the door, they heard it crash into the bushes downstairs.

He put on the deadbolt, just in case.

'What was that?' Amber asked from the sofa, voice hushed with terror.

Father Glenn had never needed to explain this to anyone before. He had to handle it delicately. He didn't want to make her hysterical again because there was only one mini-bottle of Popov left and he was saving that for himself.

'Well, it's like this,' he said. 'You inherited something from me and, to be honest, I feel a little bit guilty about it.'

'Schizophrenia?' she asked.

'How much do you know about me?' Father Glenn asked.

'That you're an asshole.' She didn't even hesitate. 'That you left when I was six. That Mom hates your guts. That you never paid child support. That you went to prison for murder.'

Father Glenn waved his hands.

'Details,' he said. 'You know anything real?'

'That you're mentally ill and passed your broken genes down to me and now I'm having a nervous breakdown.'

She just did not quit, he marvelled. Once she got the address of the complaint department she kept on sending in mail. He took a breath and focused. This was a time for honesty, that's what they always said in those mandatory prison workshops. Don't hide, don't embellish, just look people in the eye and tell them the truth.

He looked her in the eye and told her the truth.

'Amber, I see dead people.'

She didn't move for a long, long tick of the clock, then she burst out laughing. Free, easy laughter that would have been a joy to hear if it hadn't been at his expense.

'I'm sorry,' she said, seeing his serious expression. 'You really are sick in the head.'

He powered forward.

'No, I see dead people.' He tried to think of an example she'd understand. 'It's just like that poor little pudding-headed boy in the motion picture *Ghostbusters,* the one who lived next door to the space lady. Now, he saw ghosts, and they got inside him and turned him into a dog, and later on a giant marshmallow, and then they made his plant gobble up everybody, and every day it was the same thing over and over again because of the curse of that angry, underground rat, and that's my life story apart from a few minor differences. I'm a victim of supernatural forces outside my control. You see what I'm saying?'

Her face had turned grey and she shook her head from side to side.

'I don't know what you're talking about,' she moaned. 'I just want this to stop.'

'First born in every generation of our family sees ghosts,' he said. 'We all got Ghosty Vision. It kicked in for me the minute I was born, but the way I figure, you were a late bloomer and that bump on your head triggered yours.'

She looked at the coffee table, chewing her bottom lip. Realising how many shots of Popov she'd had.

'It's a concussion,' she said.

Father Glenn shook his head.

'Ghosty Vision,' he said.

'I just wanna find Mom,' she said, sounding far younger than her age.

'Now, see, sweetheart,' he said. 'That's the one thing we're not going to do. You know that fella burned up at the Denny's?'

'Brian Belovic,' she said.

'Sure,' Father Glenn agreed. 'He was cursed by a demon and sent to meet us as a booby trap.' She didn't look like she was following him. 'You know what that is?' She didn't answer. 'It's a trap the crafty Viet Cong made where they'd dig a hole and fill it with sharpened sticks and some hand grenades and you didn't see it coming. It's not specifically targeted for a woman's breasts but people call it—'

'I know what a booby trap is!' she snapped.

'Okay, okay,' he said, trying to placate her. 'Should we work out a system where if you don't know what something is, you could raise your hand so I'd know to stop and explain?'

She ignored him.

'If you see dead people, how come you didn't see anything wrong with Brian?'

He sighed.

'Because he wasn't a ghost,' he said. 'Old what's-his-name was a low-down demon worshipper, which means he'd chosen to enslave himself to the forces of darkness but he was still a normal human being.'

'Brian,' she said. 'Belovic.'

'Sure,' he said. 'That's what cursed Ryan. Some demon sent him out knowing that an individual bearing the foul word of Satan in its heart would immediately explode into cleansing flames the moment they came into contact with the Word of God.'

He held out his massive, tattoo-covered fists and flexed them.

'That was a booby trap,' he said. She started to react. 'Which you are already familiar with, I know. But the point being, your friend Stuart was cursed by a demon and sent to find someone bearing the Word of God on their body. There ain't a lot of people out there like that, and I don't think it's a coinkydink you are currently roommates with one. Using logical reason, we have to conclude that a demon from Hell now knows that I'm bunking with you, and it won't take more than a quick flip through the phonebook to figure out where that might be. And, see, sweetheart, you do not want to fuck around with demons. Ghosts are pains in the ass, but demons, they're the American Gladiators of the afterlife. There's only seven of them but they're mean motherfuckers who want to choke you out, eat your brains, and piss in your eyeholes. I don't want to tangle with any demons and neither do you.'

She stood up, agitated.

'Do you even hear yourself?' she asked. 'Demons. Ghosts. Ghosty Vision. You sound like a lunatic.'

'I didn't create this world, I just live in it,' Father Glenn said. 'And I can teach you how to live in it, too.'

'There's only one thing I want you to teach me about Ghosty Vision,' she said.

'What, sweetie?' he asked.

'How to make it go away,' she said.

They were right back at the beginning.

'You haven't been listening to me,' he said. 'It's the will of God. No take-backs, no returns. Once God turns it on there's no way to turn it off. Amen. It's part of His plan.'

She clumsily picked up the empty mini-bottles of Popov and shook them, throwing them down one after the other.

'If it's God's plan it's a stupid plan,' she said.

'Listen, now,' he said. 'I know you're no fan of my work, but this ain't the time for blasphemy. Or for personal feelings.'

'I don't have any personal feelings for you,' she said.

'But as your father—' he started.

'As my father you've passed on your mental illness to me,' she said. 'Thanks, Dad!'

'As your father,' he started again, 'I feel like you've come to the attention of a demon because of your association with me. I don't want that for you. So here's what's going to happen. We're heading for the bus station, where you need to get us two tickets to anywhere, and we both need leave town for a little while.'

'You want me to go to the bus station with you?' she slurred, the vodka finally catching up with her.

'We don't have to go someplace together,' he said. 'In fact, it's better if we don't. But right now, it's a good idea to get out of town. Okay?'

She pushed herself up off the sofa, looking angry. She reminded him of someone.

'You are *not* abandoning me and Mom again,' she said, standing too close to him, swaying.

'I'm not abandoning you,' he explained. 'I'm going to the bus station with you. And as for your mama, well, if she's still alive she's clearly with the demons now, and you'd rather stick your dick in a bull's butthole than mess with a demon.'

'If they've got Mom—' she began.

'Unh-uh,' he said. 'If they've got Mama then she's already in Hell, and I'm sorry to be the Bear of Bad News but you can't take back the rain.'

'You're just chickenshit,' she said.

He realised who she reminded him of: himself.

'Will you at least,' he asked, 'come with me to the bus station? Then you can go to Myrtle Beach, or Fort Lauderdale, or Jacksonville. Won't that be fun?'

She looked at him for a long moment, eyes narrowed.

'Please?' he asked.

She made up her mind.

'I need to pack,' she said.

He felt an enormous relief in his chest, like someone had just cracked open a bottle of Bud in his heart.

'Make it fast,' he said.

'Don't tell me what to do,' she snapped.

She stared at him. He stared at her, not sure if he'd misunderstood. She bugged her eyes out at him.

'Check!' she said.

'Check what?' he asked.

'Check my room!' she snapped. 'I'm not walking in on one of those things!'

This is what you get for not wearing a condom, Father Glenn told himself, but it was too late now. He had to play this out until she got on the bus. If he left now and she wound up in Hell with her mother he'd feel, in some small way, like it was his fault.

He checked her bedroom, then her bathroom. Because he was a professional, he even looked inside her closet.

'No ghosts,' he said, emerging from the short connecting hall.

She shoulder-checked him as she pushed by, and slammed her bedroom door.

'Don't take too long!' he called.

Then there was nothing to do but pace. So he paced. And waited. And waited and paced. He still didn't understand the remotes for the TV so he couldn't distract himself. There still wasn't any beer in the fridge so he couldn't take the edge off. He got up and listened at Amber's door but didn't hear anything.

After the day he'd had he could use a beer. His right hand still felt raw and greasy after that man burned up on him. No wonder he felt like a cat on a rocking chair. He needed a drink. He'd be doing them both a favour, frankly. A drink would straighten him out.

Before he could second guess his gut (always a mistake in his opinion) he opened her purse, lifted her wallet, slid out a twenty (and another five just in case), and padded out of the door. He had time for a quick one. Maybe two.

Across the street, The Lodge was quiet. In the first booth by the door, a guy was convincing the girl across his table that Australia was a continent, not a country. No one else was there.

Father Glenn sat down at the bar and tried to catch the eye of the hairless bartender. He arranged his body into an expectant posture. He raised his eyebrows as if he had said something and was waiting for an answer from his good friend, the bartender.

The bartender kept polishing glasses.

Father Glenn pulled out his twenty and ostentatiously placed it on the bar. The bartender slid down.

'Yeah,' he said, not a question, just a flat declaration.

'Bottle of Bud,' Father Glenn said.

He'd barely finished his sentence when the bartender had it on the bar in front of him. He pushed away Father Glenn's twenty.

'First one's on the house,' the bartender said. 'You've got character.'

Father Glenn smiled. It was nice that someone recognised his qualities. He put the twenty back in his pocket, took a sip of his Bud, and lost himself in contemplation.

He wasn't a bad man, but he did not seek out entanglements. They did not work out well for him or for the people with whom he became entangled. He preferred coming in, getting it done, and disappearing over the horizon while the gratitude of the formerly afflicted still echoed in his ears.

But here he was with a kid. And she had attracted the notice of a demon because of him. So now he had to do something about it.

He hated kids. Kids needed help with everything, and somehow everything always wound up being your fault. That's why he hadn't stuck around in the first place. Well, that and the fact that her mother had seen him less as a human being and more as a renovation project, like a human fixer-upper.

The day he'd known he'd have to leave was the day he sat down for breakfast and she put two bowls full of cardboard on the table between him and the kid. Whatever was in those bowls looked like what you'd get if a macaroni noodle fucked a rabbit pellet.

'Where's the Froot Loops?' he asked.

'It's Fibre One,' she said. 'You need to take better care of yourself. Try it.'

He did. It tasted like what you'd get if a macaroni noodle fucked a rabbit pellet. He added more milk. Now it tasted the same only wet. He put sugar on top. The same, only sugary. He was offended both for himself and for the kid. Kids should get Froot Loops. They shouldn't be forced to worry about things like their fibre intake before they were eighteen.

He looked at the kid, and to his horror saw that she was digging in as if she'd been handed a big bowl of ice cream. She looked like a little pig rooting in the tastiest shit it'd ever seen, making small happy noises. That's when he realised he needed to go. He had nothing in common with these people. If he stuck around he'd just make everyone unhappy – Sheila, the kid, himself.

Amber. She wasn't *The Kid*; she was *Amber, his daughter*.

And she was his problem now.

CHAPTER 5

AMBER SAT ON her bed, beside her open duffel bag, and waited for her hands to stop shaking. She had asked him to look in her bedroom because 'I don't want to walk in on one of those things.'

What was wrong with her? There were no things. She knew that. But he had checked, as if there were. This was bad. This was really, really bad. Why had she listened to her mom and picked him up from prison? Why hadn't she left this alone? If she had left this alone, she wouldn't be losing her mind. Again.

Ghosty Vision. Demons. Brian Belovic bursting into flames. She was slipping down that slippery slope again. She was seeing things that weren't there again. She was drinking again. It was all her dad's fault.

He threw fuel on the fire inside her brain, babbling about demons and ghosts and the Word of God. Checking her bedroom for ghosts. All that grandiose, metaphysical language she'd heard every day on the psych ward. Why was it always the people who talked about religion the loudest who left the most human wreckage in their wake?

They hadn't been big churchgoers growing up. Her mom had valued things you could see and touch. Things that would help you get a job.

'Some of the worst people I know go to church every Sunday,' she'd told Amber.

They'd volunteered at a soup kitchen every Thanksgiving, and worked at their Friends of the Library book sale. Her mom had said that working hard and helping others were what mattered, not mouthing prayers and singing hymns.

'If there is an afterlife, then everyone's there,' she'd said. 'Not just the people who go to church.'

When her mom had gone missing, she'd been frantic to find her, but no one else seemed to care. It felt like they were all moving in slow motion: the police, her mom's boss, her mom's friends from work. Everyone kept telling Amber that she'd 'turn up' or she'd 'come back' like a lost dog, and then, as the weeks passed, they began talking about how Amber needed closure, and eventually they just stopped talking to her at all. Brian Belovic was the only one who'd ever even bothered to call her back.

Her mom had said that her dad would help, but all he'd done so far was wreck her life. She remembered the last time she'd seen him. Her mom had read something online about fibre and she'd gone out and picked up a box of Fibre One because it didn't taste good but it was good for you.

'I want y'all both to be around for a long, long time,' she'd said to Amber.

The bowls hit the table and they hadn't looked good, but Amber hid her feelings because she knew how much this meant to her mom. Then she'd looked up and seen how disgusted her dad looked, staring down into his bowl like it was full of cold vomit. She'd gobbled it down and made little noises to show she enjoyed it even though it tasted like wet cardboard, hoping her mom would feel like at least one of them appreciated her effort, and maybe it would make her dad eat his, too.

Instead, her mom had gone to put the laundry in the dryer, and the second she left the room Amber watched her dad stand up, grab his jacket off the back of his chair, his cigarettes off the table, and walk out the front door. He eased the door shut behind him, rather than letting the screen slam like usual. Two minutes later her mom came back, reading the paper.

'Did your father excuse himself?' she asked, sitting down with her cup of coffee, eyes still on the headlines.

Amber shook her head.

'He go upstairs?' her mom asked, looking up now.

Amber shook her head again.

'Where is he?' her mom asked, voice tight.

Amber pointed at the front door. She would always remember the look that seeped across her mom's face. Then she threw herself towards the front door, running outside in her bathrobe and bare feet, but it was too late. She cried a lot for the rest of the year.

'He left me all alone!' she kept wailing, over and over again.

Amber had vowed never to hurt her mom like that. She had promised never to leave her alone. So when her mom had asked her to call her dad if anything ever happened to her, how could she not?

Amber had assumed prison might have changed him, made him reflect on his sins, become less of a selfish prick. She thought maybe she'd be picking up a better man who cared about what had happened to the mother of his child, who might even value reconnecting with that child, who might even help fill the gap left by her mom's disappearance.

Instead he had destroyed her life, and now he was sitting in her living room insisting she abandon everything and run away with him.

That was not going to happen.

Something rustled under her bed, soft but very, very present. Amber froze. It sounded purposeful, a sound made with intent, a slow brittle crackling like plastic bags being moved. She wasn't about to call her dad to check. Instead, she forced herself to roll over on one side and look under her bed.

A deflated dry cleaning bag lay among the dust bunnies and dim light, moving slowly towards her.

Inside she could see a baby. Through the cloudy film of synthetic polymers, she could tell it was blue.

She saw dead babies.

She didn't want to be in this room one second longer. She couldn't handle this. She pushed herself off the bed and went into her bathroom and found her pills. She took two. She wasn't supposed to just take them like this but she sometimes found that doubling up helped when the sadness got too big. When it felt like an enormous black sun pulling her up into the sky, dragging her towards its dark face, crushing her in its gravity embrace – at times like that, two pills helped.

She desperately needed to talk to someone real. She got the portable phone, sat on her closed toilet seat, opened her contact book, and dialled Dr Lin. It rang once, twice, three times, and oh, god, was it going to voicemail, she prayed it wouldn't go to voicemail, and then it got silent the way it always did when it always went to voicemail, then a man's voice said:

'Hello?'

'Dr Lin!' she almost shouted with relief, but keeping her voice down so her dad wouldn't hear. He sounded sane. He sounded like he lived in a world where no one saw dead babies. 'It's Amber.'

'Amber,' he said, and even the disappointment she heard didn't take the shine off this lifeline. 'You can't call me at home like this. Do you know what time it is?'

'I know,' she said. 'I understand. I'm sorry. But I'm seeing things again and I took my pill and I–I really think I'm having a breakdown again.'

'We have an appointment on Monday,' he said. 'Right now, you need to remember that whatever you're seeing isn't real, so it can't hurt you.'

'This is worse,' she said. 'This is so much worse than before. I made contact with my dad and maybe that triggered it, but he said some things and I think it's genetic and—'

'Amber,' he cut her off. 'We can discuss this on Monday. If you feel like you're a danger to yourself or others you have to call 9-1-1. Ask them to take you to Emory Healthcare and give them my name, okay?'

'I—'

'Amber.'

'Okay,' she said. 'Okay.'

'Strong boundaries make healthy relationships,' he said.

'Yes,' she said. 'I understand.'

He hung up. He abandoned her.

In the silence something scratched in the sand beside her. Amber made herself look down. Beside her toilet sat a litter box. One of the kind with the lid on top. She didn't have a litter box. She didn't have a cat. Inside the box, something moved in the darkness, scratched sand, bumped against the plastic wall.

She lowered herself into a squat. She made herself look through the little dark door. A headless cat with its guts hanging from its belly in loops squatted in the dimness, pooping in the middle of the phantom litter box.

She took another pill.

❧

'It's not that I feel fatherly,' Father Glenn said to the businesswoman. 'I've never had a fatherly feeling in my life.'

She nodded.

When he'd shown up half an hour ago, The Lodge had been as empty and depressing as his daughter's apartment. He figured he'd have a quick one and go, grab Amber, get a ticket to some random Florida shithole, buy her a ticket on a bus heading in the opposite direction, and be done with this episode.

But the first beer made a second one seemed like a really good idea. He hesitated, but if he wasn't planning on having a second, why had he thought of that one as his first? Before he could unravel the mystery of his own thought processes, that lady from before had come through the door in her suit and he'd made up his mind.

He needed someone to talk to, didn't he? He'd been through a lot.

He'd bought her a bourbon (Christ Almighty – eight dollars!) and asked if he could get her feminine perspective on something. She'd said of course but only if he bought her another bourbon. Well, Amber probably hadn't even finished packing yet, so he did.

Then he'd tried to sum up what he was feeling. That had required a third beer but, hell, he'd stayed one step ahead of these demonic assholes for so long, he knew he had the time for just this last quick one.

'I'm feeling, well, I don't know how to describe it,' he said, trying to put the lumpy oatmeal of his emotions into words. 'I've passed along a... genetic abnormality, and for the first time I feel, well, it's something like a sort of guilty-ish feeling.'

The businesswoman drained half her bourbon.

'I feel... responsible.' He stumbled over the word. 'Does that make sense to you? For the first time in my life I feel responsible. Is that what this is? A sense of responsibility? I think it is. I've got to admit, it ain't pleasant. But I feel like her safety, in this particular situation, is my responsibility.'

The businesswoman finished her bourbon, put down her glass, and stared him right in the eyes.

'You know what cures that feeling?' she asked.

'What?'

'Fucking,' she said.

This felt familiar. This felt safe.

'I read an article about that,' he said.

'Bathroom,' she said, standing up. 'Right now.'

Worth a shot, Father Glenn figured, and he followed her through the door marked 'Gents'.

⁂

He wanted to ruin her life, Amber realised. He wanted her to abandon the life she'd built, abandon the search for her mom, abandon her career. He wanted to make her a rootless loser, floating through America, just like him. He wanted to drag her down to his level.

Not going to happen. She was going to march right out there and tell him she wasn't going anywhere with him. He couldn't make her become a hobo. She threw open her bedroom door and stormed out into the living room.

The couch was empty. He wasn't in the kitchen. He wasn't anywhere. She felt like her mom, all those years ago: abandoned. Alone. She hated feeling like she was going to cry.

She opened her front door and stood in the breezeway, looking out over the dark street. It seemed like more people were out than usual. A car drove by and its headlights panned across a child crossing the street. No, not a child, smaller than that, and moving wrong. Was it a little person? Then she realised it was half a man. He dragged his bisected torso painfully across the asphalt, leaving a trail of his unravelling intestines behind. In the flash of headlights she saw his face, bleached of colour, mouth open in a soundless scream, eyes wide and terrified, blind with shock.

On the corner, a woman squatted against the building. She wore a rayon skirt and big hair with a shimmery polyester top and giant hoop earrings. It looked like a tasteless Halloween costume called 'Seventies Streetwalker', except for her face. It had been beaten until one half of it had caved in. The woman studied herself in the compact she held in one hand, a little sponge in the other, patting foundation onto the side of her face that wasn't a hollow crater.

They were everywhere along the street. A boy ran out of the doorway of what had been a liquor store a long time ago and was now a cheque-cashing place, holding in his guts, falling to his knees on the sidewalk, squirming soundlessly in the gutter. A suicide plunged headfirst from the building across the way, hit the sidewalk, and writhed, legs broken, ribcage shattered, pelvis cracked in half, spine twitching as he died. Someone on the corner went through the windshield of a Ford Taurus over and over again.

It was too much. Too much pain, too much sadness, too many terminal endings. Too many people who couldn't accept that they'd made their last bad decision, their ultimate closing argument, their final farewell.

Of course she hallucinated dead people everywhere. It made perfect sense. She was in mourning for her mom, so her delusions centred on death. It was a bit on the nose, to be honest, like some crappy independent film.

She missed her mom.

Everyone kept saying it would get better, but it had been ten months and she didn't feel any better. It just hurt more and more and she felt so tired all the time. Why couldn't she see her again? Just once? That's all she wanted. Just five minutes.

Down in the darkness, someone began to cry – great heaving, wracking sobs. Amber couldn't tell if they were real or inside her head, but they sounded like some lost soul, sobbing as if they'd never stop. It was more than she could take. She couldn't go through this alone. Not again. And that's what she was now. Completely and totally alone. She didn't even have a friend she could talk to. She didn't even have her mom.

She went back inside, slamming the door and locking it behind her.

❧

Father Glenn and the businesswoman were swapping spit before they even got through the bathroom door.

Father Glenn latched it behind them and when he turned around, she was already hitching up her skirt and bending over the sink.

'Hey,' Father Glenn said. 'I feel like we're really connecting here.'

She met his eyes in the graffiti-covered mirror.

'We are,' she said.

'So maybe we could do it normal?' Father Glenn said. 'And not in the poop chute this time?'

She smiled at him, a little mean, but he'd learned long ago that the kind of women who'd have sex in a bar bathroom generally had a streak of mean in them.

'Your call,' she said.

She pulled her skirt up around her waist and, as graceful as a ballerina, turned towards him and hopped up on the sink. She reached down to strip off her purple thong. He unzipped his pants, but she pushed him back by the shoulders.

'Don't you want to see what you're getting,' she purred, and now her smile didn't look mean at all. She looked randy.

Father Glenn gave her his best sexy smile and looked down at her womanly glory, ready to truly appreciate what she had to offer. His smile froze on his face.

She was nothing but scar tissue from her belly button to mid-thigh. She'd shaved her pubic hair bald and used what looked like fishing line and probably some kind of upholstery hook to sew her labia together. It looked like a pair of fat lips pressed together in disappointment.

Then she'd gone to work with a razor blade. She'd carved a pentagram around her belly button and surrounded it with runes, then upside-down crosses. Words had been carved on symbols, and symbols on top of words. He recognised some Enochian, a little Latin, some Malachim. The tissue had scarred over thick and then she'd laid on a layer of more symbols over it. Her entire bathing suit area was an enormous swirl of scars and scabs.

He wondered what she'd cut herself with, and then she raised a box cutter over her head and with a series of clicks she extended the blade and that answered his question.

'I shaved for you, Daddy,' she said, then her expression changed, like a dark blind being pulled down. 'Asmodeus says hello, Christ-fucker.'

She slashed out at his throat fast. Too fast. He didn't even see it coming.

Amber sat on her bed, writing a note on the back of a return envelope in magic marker. She'd wanted to find something more formal, but she'd been surprised to discover that she didn't have a single working pen or blank piece of paper in the entire apartment, so this would have to do.

I'm sorry, she wrote. *I can't do this again. I'm not strong enough. I'm sorry, Mom. I'm sorry, Dr Lin, I'm sorry everyone. Amber.*

She knew she could call 911. She knew she could up her dose. She knew she could go on psychiatric hold. She knew there were options. But she didn't want them anymore. She wasn't strong enough to do this alone.

Three years ago, she'd fallen off her bike taking a corner too fast and smacked her head. Even though she was wearing a helmet, they were still worried about a hairline fracture or a concussion, so the ER had sent her to get X-rayed. She'd been put in a lead apron, had some anticlimactic scanning for what felt like fifteen seconds, paid an enormous bill, and on the way home she'd seen things like she saw tonight. Hurt people. People who couldn't possibly be alive. She'd heard voices. Even when she'd locked herself in the bathroom, she could still see them in the tub. She could still hear them whispering under the door. She'd spent a month in hell. Her mom had tried to take care of her, but there was a woman standing in the corner of Amber's room, facing the wall, rocking from one foot to the other, giggling to herself all the time; and when they left her alone, she told Amber what it felt like to be dead.

She'd finally been admitted to the hospital and wound up finding Dr Lin. He started her on a course of antipsychotics and the hallucinations and voices went away after a week. Ever since, she'd lived in fear of going back there, a fear that got a little less desperate week by week, and now... she was back there.

She couldn't face this without her mom. Dr Lin hated her, and her dad was only feeding her delusions because he wanted her to be as sick as him, and she was terrified of not being able to tell what was real from what wasn't anymore.

She poured out a handful of pills and took them, one after the other, washing them down with water, and when she hit the bottle's halfway mark she lay down on her bed, hands crossed over her stomach.

She could hear the baby crinkling in its sad plastic bag beneath her. Then her bed bounced. The headless cat had hopped up and was nuzzling her feet with its neck hole. She yanked them away in revulsion.

Fuck this. It wasn't happening fast enough. She swung out of bed (checking the carpet to make sure she wasn't going to step on the baby) and opened her top dresser drawer. In one corner was a steel-blue lockbox where, on three strips of masking tape, an ex-boyfriend had written: *IN CASE OF EMERGENCY – KICK ASS.*

This was the kind of gift Keith thought made him a Good Guy. She'd held onto it after they broke up because she hadn't known how to throw a gun away. For the first time ever, she was glad she'd met Keith.

She opened the lockbox and took out the .35. She hadn't held it since that one time Keith had taken her to the range. It smelled new. It smelled good. It smelled like getting down to business. She snapped it open and started to slide in the bullets.

The dead baby rustled beneath the bed. The headless cat twined between Amber's ankles. She felt its cold guts brush her bare feet. She didn't even flinch anymore. She sat on the side of her bed, not feeling anything, holding the heavy gun in her lap. She pulled back the hammer. It took both hands. Her wrists shook with the strain. The sound was loud in the room. It sounded real.

Someone knocked on her front door.

She ignored it. She focused on the gun. On how heavy and solid it felt in her hands.

They knocked again. Fast, hard knocks like a cop.

She listened. Then something banged in her living room and she heard wood splinter. Footsteps tromped over the ruined wood of her front door. Someone was in her apartment. A lot of someones.

BAM! BAM! BAM!

Right on her bedroom door. Then again, harder.

BAM! BAM! BAM!

BAM! BAM! BAM!

Amber stood up and pointed her pistol at the bedroom door in a two-handed firing position. She'd been ready to kill herself. She wasn't ready to be murdered.

Father Glenn walked into the bar, dragging the businesswoman by her hair. He dropped her to the floor like a sack of potatoes and turned to face the crowd. They stood by their tables, they blocked the front and back doors. They all wore cheap, disposable plastic ponchos and they all carried tools: baseball bats, socket wrenches, hammers, crowbars. Even the bartender was holding a sawed-off pool cue.

'I shoulda known when I got that first beer for free,' Father Glenn said.

He raised his fists and flexed the word of God.

'Y'all want to come at me all at once, or one at a time?' he asked. 'I don't give a shit either way.'

CHAPTER 6

THE KNOCKING HAD stopped. The silence was worse. Then the doorframe splintered as Amber's bedroom door flew open so hard the knob embedded itself in the drywall. She slipped her finger through the trigger guard and raised her pistol into a classic Isosceles stance.

Three smiling men, stark naked under grey plastic ponchos, stood in the hall. They all wore shoes with dark socks. Two of them held hammers. The third had a chisel. A big one.

Amber didn't say anything. She didn't see the point. She figured the situation should explain itself.

'She has a weapon, Brother,' the man on the left observed.

'Her fear is great, Brother,' the man on the right said.

'Look thee upon the glory of Asmodeus, Sister,' the man in the middle said.

Then the three men raised their ponchos to expose their genitals, except they didn't have any. They had hacked them off long ago, and from their mid-thighs to their belly buttons they were nothing but intricate, whorling masses of scar tissue around a little ragged stump.

Amber tried to focus on the situation not the castration. She had a strong suspicion she was hallucinating. Still, Keith had been a good teacher. She held her gun steady.

The three men dropped their ponchos.

'Are you ready to meet Him, Sister?' the man in the middle asked.

❧

Father Glenn had been pushed down stairs. He'd been thrown through doors. He'd even once been shoved through a wall, leaving a hole behind shaped exactly like his body. But until tonight, he'd never been thrown through a window.

Turned out it hurt. A lot.

He remembered being lifted and then he was flying weightless through the air, not knowing where to put his feet, nothing to hold onto, not knowing which way was up, and then his brain calculated the geography of The Lodge and he thought, *I shouldn't be flying this far, unless I'm about to go through that plate glass window.*

Then he went through that plate glass window.

The noise was enormous. He landed on the sidewalk, knocking the air out of his lungs, ears ringing, enormous shards of glass falling around him like guillotine blades, trying to stand up, slipping on broken glass. He staggered, he stood, he stumbled into the middle of the street, then he managed to focus his blurry vision on the front of The Lodge. The Disciples of Asmodeus crowded the doorway and the hole where the window had been.

'Dirty fighters!' Father Glenn shouted, then he ducked at the gunshots he heard behind him. He turned, just in time to hear another one and see muzzle flash in the window of his daughter's apartment.

Amber had made a decision based on logic and evidence. Dr Lin would be proud.

'You're not real,' she said to the first man on the left and pulled the trigger the way she'd done that long-ago day on the range. The pistol exploded. Half the man's head sheared off and painted the doorjamb behind him in thick red paste. He went straight down.

The other two men started walking towards her, casually stepping over his body. That probably meant they also weren't real.

'You don't exist, either,' she said, and shot the second man twice in the chest. He flew backwards and hit the wall with a thud that reverberated through the apartment.

Amber took aim at the third man, who was still coming.

'You're a byproduct of a chemical imbalance in my brain,' she explained, then pulled the trigger three times.

The man spun sideways, smashing his face on the corner of her dresser as he went down. Gunsmoke hung in the air. Another man stepped into her doorway. Without thinking, Amber aimed and pulled the trigger.

'Whoa!' Father Glenn said, sitting down hard on the carpet.

The firing pin snapped dry, the hammer coming down on empty chambers. Amber stood there, gun out, while Father Glenn took in the room.

'Nice shooting, Tex,' he said.

Behind him he heard feet thundering up the stairs, he felt the building shake, he heard bare feet storming down the breezeway. He pushed himself off the floor and saw that he didn't even have time to get the front door locked and blocked before they got swarmed. He saw the window at the other end of the room. Twice in one night? Did he have it in him?

Did he have a choice?

Amber looked at the dead bodies on her bedroom floor and wondered why they hadn't disappeared. For hallucinations, they were awfully realistic. She had a thought. It didn't feel good. She turned to her dad.

'Are these real people?' she asked.

In the living room, feet stampeded through the shattered front door. Father Glenn led Amber over and stood her in front of her bedroom window. The pills were starting to take effect and she felt slow and her joints were full of jelly.

'You ever jumped out a second-storey window before?' Father Glenn asked.

'Whaaaa...?' she asked in slow motion.

'You take something?' he asked, stripping the comforter off her bed and throwing it over her head.

Her tongue felt thick and dry, her lips felt numb.

'I didun' wan' live lieee' thisss...' she managed to say.

'Hold tight,' Father Glenn said, then took a running start and tackled Amber out the second-storey window of her apartment.

They fell for what felt like forever and landed on the grass. Father Glenn rolled and came up, realised nothing was broken, and allowed himself a single fist pump.

'Booyah!' he shouted.

He yanked the comforter off Amber, sprawled bonelessly in the grass.

'Whaaaa?' she asked, trying to sit up, slowly shaking her head.

Father Glenn squatted in front of her and stared into her eyes. He couldn't see her pupils. He squeezed her earlobe and simultaneously pinched the skin between her thumb and her forefinger. Hard.

Her eyes cleared, snapping into focus.

'What did you do?' she asked. 'What did I do?'

Above them, faces of the Disciples filled the broken bedroom window. Lights started snapping on all over the apartment complex. Father Glenn heard running feet down the street, coming around corners from all sides, getting closer, people shouting orders up and down the block.

'Reflexology,' he told his daughter, then grabbed her hand and pulled her to her feet.

He yanked Amber behind him as they ran, and she ran faster to keep up. All around him he saw poncho maniacs converging on them out of the dark, but he and Amber still had a clear path to the street. A car came around the far corner and Father Glenn ran faster, hoping to make it. He lost a flip-flop and let go of Amber's hand and ran into the middle of the road, waving his arms back and forth, flagging the driver down. They needed a ride out of this mess.

Instead of slowing down, the car sped up, pinning him in its headlights, blinding him, and he didn't know which way to run, so he listened to his gut and did something he hadn't done in twenty-three years. At the last minute, he dove forward, planting his hands on the hood of the car, flipping his legs up into the air, feeling his joints creak, letting the velocity pick him up and carry him along, rolling up the windshield and over the roof of the car, falling through space and landing, hard, on the street. He peeled himself up off the asphalt.

'Oh my god!' Amber said, running to him.

'Oh my God!' Father Glenn said in agony.

He'd lost his other flip-flop.

Disciples poured out of the darkness on either side of the street.

'Bus!' Amber shouted and now she was pulling him and he stumble-ran with her and he saw what she was dragging him towards: a brightly lit city bus, idling at a bus stop down the block.

Bare feet pounded asphalt behind them.

'Wait!' Amber yelled as the two of them sprinted for the bus.

The thundering feet got closer, and then they were at the taillights of the bus, alongside it, the doors were closing, and...

They made it. Amber swiped her pass. The driver held out an arm.

'Where's his?' he asked, pointing at Father Glenn.

Amber looked. The Disciples were at the back bumper of the bus now, halfway up, almost to the door.

Without hesitation, she flashed the driver her breasts. The bus driver nodded and pulled the door closed, just as the first Disciple slammed into it. The bus pulled out, and as Amber led Father Glenn to a seat in the middle of the empty bus, they heard the enraged Disciples slapping their hands against the sides as it pulled away.

'Some people,' the driver said in disgust.

⁂

They sat, huddled together in the shadows, on a bench outside the police station. On the one hand, it felt safe to be surrounded by cops, by cop cars, by the occasional conversation between cops wandering down the sidewalk with coffees. On the other hand, it gave Amber time to think. Time to realise that she had shot and most likely seriously injured (if not killed) three human beings. And she'd jumped out a window. Well, to be honest, she had been thrown. And she had flashed her boobs to a bus driver. And she was losing her mind.

But she hadn't lost her sense of right and wrong. She stood up.

'I'm going to turn myself in,' she said.

Father Glenn yanked her back down so hard it wrenched her shoulder. Although, to be fair, every part of her hurt.

'Shut up,' he hissed.

'People tried to kill me,' she said.

'Keep it down,' he hissed, louder.

'I killed people,' Amber said, more quietly.

'They weren't people,' Father Glenn said.

For a moment, Amber felt a wave of relief wash over her, then she considered the source of this information.

'No,' she said. 'I'm pretty sure they were people.'

He stopped scanning the darkness and fixed her with a look.

'You can't think of them as human,' he said.

'They were human beings,' she said, feeling her throat closing up at the enormity of what she'd done. 'With families and children and pets.'

'Asmodeus cultists,' he said. 'They're, like, the biggest nerds in Hell. They can't please a woman between the sheets so they make up for it by being bloodthirsty lunatics in the streets.'

How could he sound so confident? He didn't know who these people were.

'They were still human beings,' she said. 'With lives.'

'To join the cult of Asmodeus,' he said. 'You have to renounce your family and turn your back on the world. Renouncing your family's no big deal, everyone's done that at some point. But the Disciples are real assholes about it. They prefer if you don't leave any survivors. Then you have to kill someone, usually a drifter, someone living rough, someone the cops don't care about, and you have to do it in an unpleasantly sexual way. They take pictures so they'll always have something to use against you if you ever try to leave. Every single one of those people you shot has done something horrible to some innocent person, probably while laughing their heads off or singing in close harmony.'

As deranged as it sounded, it did make her feel a little better. He was a lying scumbag but he seemed to know about this stuff.

'I thought I was going crazy,' Amber said. 'I was about to kill myself.'

She figured he wouldn't care, so she jumped a little when something touched her hand. She looked down. His hand rested awkwardly on top of hers.

'No shame in that,' he said. 'Demonic forces get involved and the human brain goes haywire. I'd say you're handling it pretty well, the Ghosty Vision and what-not.'

'I am?' she asked.

'I was a basket case,' he said. 'Saw them from the day the doctor dropped me on my head at five minutes old. I didn't even start talking until I was five years old because I didn't want them to hear me.'

She felt an unexpected pang for the child he'd been.

'That must've been horrible,' she said.

'I used to take the time to lay them to rest,' he said. 'Send them to Heaven with a prayer, but it was so much work and there were so many of them that I stopped after a while. They never said thank you anyways.'

Father Glenn jumped in alarm and yanked his hand back as voices emerged from the shadows. Two cops in blue uniforms walked by, chatting away. One of them carried a clear plastic bag from Subway. They stopped talking as they passed Father Glenn and Amber, giving them the side eye, evaluating them as potential threats, then they were past, picking up their conversation again, walking through the automatic sliding glass doors into the police station.

'Can't we talk to the cops?' she asked.

'No.'

'We need a plan.'

'This is the plan,' he said.

'This is vagrancy.'

'Plans are how they find you,' he said. 'Routines and schedules and fixed permanent addresses are for normal people. You're not normal people anymore.'

'No,' she said. 'I'm a normal person who's been dragged into some kind of bizarre world that you seem way too comfortable with. I want to go back to my real life.'

'That's the plan,' he said. 'But we've got to do it my way.'

'Why are they even chasing us?' she asked. 'Does it have anything to do with Mom?'

'The Seven Major Demons mostly stay in Hell, but I know Asmodeus real good,' Father Glenn said, going back to scanning the dark. 'And I'll tell you what, he is one humourless prick.'

Suddenly it all made sense to Amber.

'What did you do?'

'I'm not the bad guy here,' Father Glenn protested, his voice suddenly high-pitched with indignation. 'He's a demon from Hell! I'm your daddy. You need to be on my side. Besides, this is on you. I got noticed by these malignant powers a long time ago, and going to the cooler got me unnoticed. My guess is they were watching you to see if I'd show up again and you led them right to me. And I'm going to tell you what, Asmodeus is slow, he is patient, and he won't stop looking for me, ever. And neither will his fanboys.'

'Mom's not a part of this?' she asked. 'Is she?'

'No,' he said, confidently. 'Asmodeus is the Demon of Lust. That's why his fanboys chop off their peckers. He's got nothing to do with your mama. If one of them said something to you to the contrary, just remember the source: they're demon-worshipping lunatics.'

'Then why'd Mom want me to get you?'

'That is a mystery,' Father Glenn said. 'But I'm glad she did. It's good to have gotten a look at you, because we're never going to see each other again.'

Her back stiffened. One more rejection tonight was more than she could take, even from him.

'Fine by me,' she said.

'Aw, sweetheart,' he said. 'It's not you, it's me. I can't be around you or your mama. I've got pretty much all seven of the Major Demons looking to torture me for eternity. That makes it hard for me to have normal human relationships. But you can learn to ignore the ghosts, ignore everything, and be normal. Forget your mama, forget me, and the demons'll leave you alone as long as you keep your head down and I stay away. I want you to have a normal life.'

'Why do you even care?' she asked.

''Cause I never got one,' he said.

They sat with that quietly for a moment.

'There's one fella who can help us,' Father Glenn said. 'And come sun-up we'll go see him. But till then we're sitting tight in the lap of the Atlanta PD, clinging to them like a baby monkey on his mama's tit.'

Suddenly she felt like they were too exposed, that there were too many approaches, too many ways for those men in grey ponchos to come running out of the dark.

'We need to get off the street,' she said, half to herself, looking around, wondering what she had in her wallet, and if it was enough to get them a room. Two rooms. Had she maxed out her cards this month?

'This entire building is full of cops,' Father Glenn said. 'They'll beat a man to death just for breathing funny.'

'No,' Amber said, a cold sweat prickling her scalp. 'We need to do the smart thing.'

'We are,' he said.

She shook her head so hard her hair flew around her face.

'Listen,' she said. 'I don't trust you about pretty much anything, but so far the one thing I do trust you on, one hundred per cent, is this freaky, weird, sick occult stuff. But trust is a two-way street, and if I'm trusting you about demons from Hell and homicidal cultists, you need to trust me on the normal, everyday things, like paying your bills, and not walking out on your family, and staying out of prison.'

She stared at him, clearly expecting an answer.

'Okay?' he said hesitantly, because he had a feeling this was leading somewhere he didn't want to go.

She stood up.

'And one of those everyday things,' she said, 'is that you go to the police when you're in trouble. Now, come on.'

She marched through the police station doors and stopped, waiting for him.

'Dammit,' Father Glenn muttered to himself. 'Why doesn't anybody ever listen to me?'

But he got up off the bench and followed her inside.

CHAPTER 7

THE LOBBY LOOKED more like the lobby of a private high school than the gateway to The System. Under its bright lights, surrounded by upbeat motivational posters and framed photographs of smiling officers playing volleyball with children in wheelchairs, Amber felt more confident. She strode to the man she assumed was the receptionist. Or whatever you called a cop receptionist.

'Hi,' she said, pulling out her driver's licence. 'My name's Amber Lieberman. My father and I were attacked by a gang of people earlier this evening.'

'That's terrible,' the cop said in a surprisingly sympathetic voice. 'Are either of you hurt?'

'No,' Amber said, impressed by his sincerity. 'Thank you for asking, though. You don't know how much I appreciate that.'

'Do you know who your assailants were?' he asked.

Amber took a breath. This was the moment she'd been dreading, but she didn't see a way around it.

'They were some kind of a religious cult,' she said, and waited.

'That is the worst,' the cop said. 'When crazed religious cultists start attacking people it gives religion a bad name. I'm a Lutheran, myself.' Then he turned and called, 'Pete! Charlie! Come here for a minute!'

Two officers in summer suits looked over, then approached the desk.

'What's up?' the younger-looking of the two asked.

'This young woman and her father were attacked by religious cultists,' the desk officer said.

'Oh no!' the younger detective said.

'That's terrible,' the older detective said.

He had genuinely kind eyes.

'Can you take their statements?' the desk officer asked. 'Seriously, if a bunch of theologically delinquent lunatics are running around on the streets, we need as much information about them as we can get.'

Amber felt relieved that they were being taken seriously. This was an experience that felt familiar, turning herself over to a larger system, letting its rules and experts take charge, guiding her to where she needed to be.

Pete and Charlie led her and her dad deep into a maze of cubicles until they reached a conference room. The younger one turned out to be Pete. The older one with the kind eyes was Charlie. They were both Very Concerned.

'So what happened?' Charlie asked, pen poised above a yellow legal pad.

Amber looked at her father but he didn't look like he was going to say a word.

'Well,' she said, trying to think of ways to make it sound more reasonable. 'We were minding our own business in my apartment, and out of nowhere these three crazy men in ponchos kicked in the door and attacked us.'

'You were minding your own business,' Charlie said, writing. 'Not bothering anyone, not being provocative...'

'Definitely not,' Amber said.

'...and they just kicked down your door and came at you?' Pete finished.

'Yeah,' Amber said. 'They had hammers and stuff like that. I, um, I actually shot one, no, three of them.'

'In your home?' Pete asked as Charlie furiously filled the legal pad.

'Yes,' Amber said.

'Well,' Pete said. 'There're all kinds of protections in the state of Georgia for a licenced gun owner to protect their home.'

Amber felt her heart overflow with relief.

'Do you know what kind of religious cult it was?' Charlie asked, looking up. 'Mormon? Mennonite? Polyamorous?'

'Um.' Amber didn't know how to say this exactly. 'Ass Modey Us?'

The words felt alien in her mouth.

'Asmodeus,' her dad said, speaking for the first time. 'The Cult of Asmodeus.'

Pete and Charlie gave each other a baffled look.

'Never heard of that one,' Charlie said.

'Me neither,' Pete said, then hastened to reassure Amber. 'But that doesn't mean they're not bad news.'

'Absolutely,' Charlie said. 'In fact, it might even mean they're worse.'

'Exactly,' Pete said. 'A new cult might feel like they've got more to prove.'

'Do you want to ride with us over to your apartment?' Charlie asked. 'You can show us the scene and we can see what happened ourselves.'

'Not that we don't trust you,' Pete said.

'Absolutely,' Charlie said. 'Just we're trained professionals, so we might catch something you missed.'

'I'd really rather not go back there,' Amber said. 'I mean, I want to do anything I can to help you guys but it was pretty terrifying.'

As she said 'terrifying' Pete's pager went off. He checked the number and punched it into a phone on the other end of the conference table.

'Detective Bruner,' he said. 'Uh-huh... uh-huh... plastic ponchos?' He pulled Charlie's pad over and studied it. 'Mutilated genitals? Oh boy. I'll ask.' He held the phone away from his ear. 'Did the cultists who attacked the two of you have mutilated genitals? I mean, I hate to even ask.'

'They did,' Amber said.

Pete put the phone back to his ear.

'Okey dokey,' he said. 'Sounds like a match. We'll be right over.'

He hung up.

'You won't believe who that was,' he said. 'That was Westside. They just arrested a bunch of guys in ponchos with mutilated genitals who were running down the street carrying hammers, hand axes, all kinds of very dangerous weapons. They picked them up on general principle, but they were wondering if we had anyone who could come down and ID them or maybe file charges.'

There was a long moment in the room.

'You know,' Charlie said, 'if I wrote a book about my life, people would say I was making it up.'

❦

The smooth saxophone and electronic percussion of Kenny G's 'Silhouette' filled the unmarked car as they glided through the Atlanta streets. Out the windows, the late-night sidewalks were empty, and the McMansions were dark. Father Glenn sat in the back with Pete while Amber rode shotgun beside Charlie. Both the cops kept up a slick line of patter which Father Glenn found annoying.

'The issue with religious cults is their niche appeal,' Pete said from beside Father Glenn. 'Hence the name, "cults", like "cult movie", or "cult classic". They're embraced by a very passionate but limited group of enthusiasts.'

They turned onto yet another empty Atlanta street. In the distance, an SUV rolled through an intersection. On the radio, Kenny G sent his soprano sax scrambling up the scales into overdrive. But not too much overdrive.

'Agreed,' Charlie said from behind the wheel. 'Although you can't argue the fact that many of the world's great religions started out as so-called cults.'

Their practised back-and-forth, probably honed over hundreds of hours sitting in unmarked cars watching drug drops, made Father Glenn feel drowsy.

'Point taken,' Pete said, amiably.

Amber's head nodded on the end of her neck, then snapped back up.

'How far is the Westside Precinct?' Father Glenn asked, his voice sounding too loud in their comfortable lite-jazz capsule.

'Far,' Charlie said from the front seat. 'All the way over on the west side.'

'They serve a more suburban community,' Pete explained. 'I want to transfer there one day.'

The McMansions grew further apart, highway on-ramps grew more frequent, then less frequent, then they were on a highway passing dark used car lots and closed Hardees. The anonymous retail landscape hypnotised Father Glenn. So it was a shock when the vehicle actually made a turn.

'Ding ding!' Charlie cheered from the front seat. 'End of the line!'

The car bounced over dirt, sending Father Glenn's head snapping back and forth as they pulled around a dumpster on the side of a construction site and Charlie shifted into park and shut off the car. The engine ticked and cooled.

Beside them, something dark loomed against the night sky. It took Father Glenn a minute to realise it was a building under construction, maybe an office park or a medical billing facility. It had been framed but its sides remained open.

'Where's the station?' Amber asked.

'They're repaving their parking lot so we're coming in from the back,' Pete said, as Charlie got out and the interior light turned on, bathing them in its sick yellow glow.

He opened Amber's door, then Pete's, and Father Glenn slid out, flexing his stiff butt muscles. They stood in loose dirt, strewn with scrap lumber and piles of rusty rebar.

'This way,' Pete said, leading them around the side of the framed building. 'Watch out for nails.'

Amber followed Pete, with Father Glenn right behind and Charlie bringing up the rear.

'It's being renovated to make it more community friendly,' Pete said.

'Community-based models of policing really are the future,' Charlie said.

The dull orange glow of the streetlights barely reached back here. Piles of lumber cut them off from the street. Pete came to a stop and somehow Amber and Father Glenn wound up standing side by side, facing them. Father Glenn looked for the police station, or a parking lot, or any other human beings, but he didn't see a single sign of life.

'Now,' Charlie said. 'If you guys would do us a huge favour, could you kneel down facing away from us?'

'It sounds strange, but to be honest,' Pete said, 'we don't want to have to look you in the eyes.'

'Wait a minute...' Amber said, but her voice sounded thick and confused.

Pete literally smacked himself in the forehead.

'Charlie,' he said. 'We are the rudest idiots.'

He walked away into the shadows and came back with two empty paper bags. He folded them up and laid them on the ground, one behind Amber, the other behind Father Glenn.

'Of course, you don't want you to get your pants dirty,' Pete said.

'Those are some great slacks.' Charlie grinned at Amber.

'Thank you,' Amber said, automatically, then shook her head like a cartoon character. 'Wait a second. No. What's going on here?'

'Just kneel facing away from us,' Charlie said.

'No, Charlie,' Pete said. 'No, they deserve an explanation. You see, we brought you here under false pretences, and for that we are truly sorry. But both Charlie and I felt you would have been extremely distressed to know that we were bringing you here to shoot you in the backs of your heads.'

'You would have been upset about it,' Charlie said. 'But since your deaths are inevitable that would have been pointless.'

The two cops smiled sheepishly. They looked goofy, but Father Glenn was extremely aware of the brown holsters and heavy black pistols strapped to their belts. He had no doubt they'd happily shoot them the instant they ran.

Amber turned her confused, blank face from one of them to the other.

'You're kidding, right?' she said, smile fading.

Father Glenn felt furious with himself. If he'd stuck with his gut and not listened to his daughter they wouldn't be about to get shot right now.

'It's important to remember that we're not killing you,' Charlie said.

'Oh, good Lord, no,' Pete said. 'Think of us as putting you to sleep like beloved family pets.'

'Although,' Charlie amended, 'I would take my Tinkerbelle to a veterinarian if I was going to euthanise her, not to an abandoned construction site.'

'Of course,' Pete said, lapsing into their familiar rhythm. 'I'd have it done in a clean and hygienic setting. Not here. This place is filthy.'

Father Glenn tried to think of his next move, tried to formulate an escape, but the thoughts wouldn't connect in his head. He used to be so good at this. Then he realised the problem: he'd never had to think for two before.

'Now,' Charlie said, unsnapping his holster and drawing his pistol. It looked enormous in his hand. 'Please kneel? And don't make me raise my voice. I hate raising my voice.'

'He really does,' Pete said, unsnapping his pistol. 'It's one of his pet peeves.'

They didn't need to threaten. The guns in their hands made the consequences pretty explicit. Amber turned her back on them, and shakily kneeled first, facing into the night. Then they turned their combined attention on Father Glenn. He didn't sense any other way forward, and so, furious with himself for being in this position, and frustrated he had no other ideas, he slowly turned and knelt, knees popping.

'I should have known,' he said as he went down, trying to hold onto some dignity. 'Cops are never this nice.'

The paper bag crinkled beneath his knees.

'That's an unfair stereotype,' Charlie protested.

'We're the nicest two cops you'll ever meet,' Pete added.

'You're about to shoot us in the head,' Amber pointed out.

Pete didn't miss a beat.

'But we're being very nice about it.'

Something digital shimmered in the air. It sounded out of place. Then it repeated itself. Pete and Charlie's attention shifted from Father Glenn and Amber.

'You should get that,' Charlie said to Pete.

Pete reached into his suit jacket with his free hand and pulled out a cellular phone. He flipped it open and held it to one ear.

'Hello?' he asked.

He took a few steps away and turned a shoulder for privacy. Charlie focused his attention on the call, trying to decode from his partner's back what was happening. His gun, however, remained on Amber and Father Glenn.

'I hate you,' Amber whispered.

'I'm the one who wanted to stay outside,' Father Glenn hissed back.

'I really, really hate you,' Amber whisper-hissed, and her voice hitched like she was about to cry.

Something about it, the little girl sound, reminded Father Glenn of when she'd been a kid, a long time ago, and it activated some need inside of him to provide comfort. They were both about to die in the dirt for reasons he didn't understand, at least he could administer some emotional anaesthetic to this kid.

'I made a lot of mistakes in my life,' he said. 'But I left you and your mama to protect you from situations exactly like this, because they happen to me on a pretty regular basis. You do the work I do and you attract random outbreaks of violence and all kinds of fucked-up supernatural shit.'

He had her attention.

'I should have walked in the other direction the second I came out of those prison gates,' he said. 'And kept you away from my life. But the second I saw you I thought this might be my chance to make things right.'

'You thought I was a hooker,' Amber hissed at him, and he thought that wasn't entirely fair.

'I thought it might be my chance to make things right,' Father Glenn whispered back. 'And maybe get a handjob. You can't blame a recently released con for that. But the second I realised you were my daughter, I didn't want the handjob anymore. And I want you to know, this last day, seeing how good you've turned out, well, it's been the best day of my life in over a decade. And I'm not even thinking about the handjob anymore, to be honest.'

There, he told himself. *That ought to bring her some peace.*

'In the past twenty-four hours,' Amber whispered, 'I have watched a man burn to death, had a nervous breakdown, almost killed myself, murdered three people, and now I'm kneeling in the dirt about to get shot in the head by two very polite psychopaths because I trusted you. So I'd like to say, for the record, that this has been the absolute worst day of my life.'

Pete snapped his phone shut and rejoined them.

'We good?' Charlie asked.

'Sterling,' Pete said.

'Why are you doing this?' Amber asked.

The two cops looked down at them in surprise. They exchanged a look.

'We aren't doing anything,' Pete said. 'You've got it backwards. We are simply tools executing His Will.'

'Humble servants,' Charlie said, bowing his head. 'In the great work.'

Amber looked at her father, her face wearing an expression that said, *You have got to be kidding me.*

'The rage of the Wrathful One flows through us,' Pete said, his voice getting louder and not a little bit ranty. 'The Great Horned Dragon. The Burning Hammer of Apocalypse. The Beast Wormwood. Our King. Our Redeemer. The Enraged Master...'

Charlie joined him on the chorus as they chanted together, 'Hail Satan, the God of Retribution and Woe! Hail, Our Dark Lord and Master.'

'I should've known,' Father Glenn spat. 'Satanists.'

The metallic, well-oiled sound of thumbs drawing back the hammers of two service revolvers was loud in the night air.

'I'd suggest you both close your eyes,' Charlie suggested.

Father Glenn felt time contract, his life narrowing down to this one moment. It seemed awfully unfair. He'd had a fascinating and unusual life. He'd never wasted much time thinking about how it would end but he'd always assumed it would be better than this. More dramatic, more comfortable, more meaningful. Maybe with a handjob?

'Gentlemen,' a voice called, cutting through the dark.

It came from far outside their circle. Father Glenn opened his eyes and turned. Pete and Charlie were looking around, trying to see where it came from. Then they locked onto a calm-looking man wearing a navy blue double-breasted suit standing behind them. He looked cool, unruffled, and one hundred per cent blow-dried.

'Excuse me, sir,' Charlie said, a bit of rudeness in his voice. 'Police business.'

The man started to walk towards them.

'I believe these two need to come with me,' he said, smiling.

'Don't make him raise his voice,' Pete said. 'He really hates doing that.'

'That's all right,' the man said, and he was halfway to them by now.

To Father Glenn's relief, Pete and Charlie turned their guns on the stranger. It felt like overkill for this one lost businessman, but he seemed unconcerned.

'I hate to sound authoritarian,' Pete said, 'but stop right there. The threat of violence is implied.'

'Thank you for all your hard work, officers,' the man said, stopping right there, about five feet away. 'But we no longer require your assistance.'

'It's my belief,' Charlie said, 'that you have drastically misread the situation.'

Unbelievably, the man's smile got bigger.

'Then we're reading very different books,' he purred, his voice like silk.

He gestured airily around him with one hand, like a tour guide on a European sightseeing trip, directing their attention around the construction site to various points of interest, like the young man in a power tie and suspenders standing behind the dumpster with an assault rifle held against his shoulder, pointed at them. Or the woman in a red skirt and jacket on the second floor of the framed building, also pointing a large piece of military hardware in their direction. To their far left, a woman in a sporty, yellow, polka-dotted pantsuit stood, holding what Father Glenn recognised from movies as an Uzi.

'Why don't you walk away,' the businessman said with a light chuckle. 'And we'll take it from here?'

'No, thank you,' Charlie said.

'This is very awkward,' Pete said.

'Well,' the man said. 'Maybe we could review our options.'

The night tore open as flashes of fire sprung from the machine guns and gunfire ripped up the dark. Everything strobed as a stuttering sound hammered their brains in stereo, making it hard to think. Amber threw herself forward, face down in the dirt, tasting grit in her mouth. She tried to press herself into the ground as bullets chainsawed the air above her. She could feel the percussive blasts of steady machine-gun fire across her back, vibrating her ribs.

She had to get away from this noise, she had to get somewhere safe. She dragged herself forward on her elbows, powered by a primal urge to hide from the bad sounds. Her world narrowed down to dragging herself through the dirt. She didn't care about anything but getting away. Getting safe. Getting out. She was so focused on moving forward that she didn't even notice the noises stop. She just kept crawling until she ran into a pair of freshly shined thousand-dollar loafers.

'Hello,' the man said above her. Amber looked up. He looked down and smiled. Her ears rang. 'I imagine you have a lot of questions. I'll give you a lift and we can chat.'

Amber sat up. She looked back. Two bodies, which she assumed were the cops, lay in the dirt. One of them seemed to be missing quite a lot of his skull.

'I'll walk,' she said, feeling a giddy sense of relief.

He helped her up. His skin felt cool, almost cold, to the touch.

'Oh,' he said. 'I'm sorry. You're mistaking my offer for a request.'

Amber brushed dirt from her clothes. She couldn't stand all these people and their arch dialogue.

'Dad?' she asked. 'Who the hell are these assholes?'

He didn't answer, and she had a sinking feeling. She turned.

'I believe,' the smooth-talking man said, 'that your father has taken advantage of the confusion to make his exit.'

More men and women emerged from the darkness around them, wearing business casual and carrying the kind of heavy calibre weapons Amber had only ever seen in news segments on foreign wars.

'Search,' the man snapped and immediately they faded into the shadows, trotting towards the treeline, disappearing into the half-built building.

Amber realised there was nowhere to go. They had the guns, they called the shots. She didn't have anything to bargain with, she didn't even have a basic understanding of the situation. All she had was her dad, and with every passing second she realised she might not even have that.

Headlights swept across the construction site, showing her that it was now swarming with people who looked like they should be carrying folders around an office, not giant black machine guns around a filthy half-built office park. A stretch limo pulled off the road and dragged itself over the dirt, bouncing over ruts, coming towards them as slow and implacable as a tank, closer and closer until it was closer than Amber deemed wise. Then it stopped, engine purring.

Something clutched her hand and pulled, and she looked and saw that the businessman had dropped to his knees and bowed his head. He pulled her down beside him. Her knees landed painfully in the dirt. Right on a nail.

One of the well-dressed yuppies opened the rear door and the limo rocked from side to side as something large, maybe the entire back passenger seat, pushed its way out. It moved away from the limo and Amber realised it was a man, an obese man the size of a large sofa, shuffling through the dirt, using two canes.

The closer he got, the more Amber saw: his immaculate three-piece suit, his wide red tie, little wisps of smoke rising off his back and shoulders as if a banked fire lurked deep within his body. The only sound was his breathing, wet and liquid, wheezing with the effort of each painful step. Finally he stood over her. It hurt her neck to look up at him. He was massive, filling her field of vision like a Brooks Brothers planet.

'Ah,' he said, in a high-pitched voice that seemed out of proportion to his size. 'The daughter. Much prettier in person.'

She swallowed her automatic need to thank him for the compliment.

'We can't find him,' a young man holding some kind of complicated rifle said, coming up behind the enormous man and bowing his head, addressing his feet. 'Should we search the woods?'

'You don't ever "find" a human,' the big man said. 'You make them come to you.'

Then slowly, painfully, he bent down to Amber's level, holding onto his two canes for dear life. His knuckles creaked and his wrists shook.

'We are,' he said, as if he were introducing himself at a cocktail party, 'Volker & Leeman, Attorneys at Law.'

He saw the recognition in her eyes.

'Yes, your mother's law firm. We wish to locate your father and you will help us do that, or I will tear your womb from your body with my bare hands and make you watch me eat it. After that, we would still find your father, it would take longer and I would be in a worse mood.'

Amber felt the knowledge fill her. Everything led here. This man was the wizard behind the curtain, the end of the road.

'You're Asmodeus,' she said.

He surprised her by laughing a delicate, tinkling laugh.

'Your father has left you woefully unprepared,' he said, then took an enormous breath and pushed himself upright.

The effort made him unleash a long, greasy fart. It smelled like something that had recently died.

'Please,' he said. 'Allow Derick to introduce myself.'

He began to limp back to his limousine as the businessman kneeling beside Amber, whom she assumed was Derick, began shouting.

'Hail!' Derick shouted. 'Hail, Belphegor!'

Across the construction site, young men and women who looked like the kind of people you met at sales conventions chanted along with him.

'Hail, Lord of the Flies!' they shouted. 'Hail, O Winged One, King of Shit, Future Ruler of Hell.'

Amber felt herself leave reality firmly and fully behind as she floated off into space. She was kneeling in a construction site, having seen and committed more murder in one evening than she had ever thought she'd witness in her entire life. Her father had abandoned her with these Satanists, or whatever the Hell they were, before he ran away to save himself.

'Has my dad managed to piss off absolutely everyone in the world?' she asked Derick.

He turned his eyes to her. They looked very kind.

'Will you help us find him?' he asked.

She laughed, a short, cynical bark.

'Do I have any choice?' she said. 'You're the ones with the guns.'

He helped her to her feet.

'We're not looking for a victim,' he said, earnestly. 'We seek a partner.'

Amber looked at the two paper bags spread on the dirt, the one where she had knelt and the one where her father had knelt beside her. She could see the twin impressions made by his knees, before he abandoned her. Again.

She had trusted him because he'd sounded so sincere, and it had almost gotten her killed. The same way her mom had trusted him years ago, and now she was missing and, let's face it, probably dead. He was poison. He was radioactive. He destroyed everything he touched. She'd bent over backwards for him and the only thing she'd accomplished was almost dying. Also, a man had been set on fire.

She looked around the construction site. These well-dressed, well-mannered people may be demon-worshippers, but they seemed to really and truly hate her father. Almost as much as she did. To her, that sounded like a good place to start.

'Let's talk in the car,' she said, smiling at Derick.

The convoy left the construction site, luxury sedans peeling off in all directions when they reached the street, until Derick and Amber were driving alone in his Saab. Neither spoke. The soft sound of Bach drifted from the CD player.

Amber examined Derick out the side of her eyes. He had healthy cuticles. His shave was perfect: no nicks, no razor burn, no extra hairs peeking from his nostrils. He caught her looking.

'I'm a normal human being,' he said. 'Just like you.'

'No,' she said. 'You cost more.'

'$320 an hour,' he said, turning right.

'Doing what?' she asked.

'Corporate law.'

Even though Amber's entire body hurt, a bit of hysteria slipped out.

'That's a bit on the nose,' she giggled.

'What?' he asked, merging onto the highway.

'Demonic lawyers,' she said.

He smoothly picked up speed, hands on the wheel at ten and two.

'"Demon" is such a pejorative term,' he said. 'We prefer "theologically different". Belphegor, all hail His name, is one of the seven Princes of Hell. It's like working for any boss with a royal title, except he happens to be thousands of years old and has a particular interest in the ruination of all mankind.'

'Theologically different?' she asked. 'Isn't that like calling Hitler "ethically challenged"?'

He made a harsh sound.

'Bzzt. You lose. I'm invoking the Nazi Rule.'

He put on his blinker and glided off the highway.

'Fine,' she said, having invoked it on her ex-boyfriend, Keith, all the time: the second you use Nazis as an example, you've lost the argument. 'But what I've learned tonight is that people like me tend to get guns pointed at them when demons are involved.'

'The only thing you know about theologically complex individuals like Belphegor is what you've read in the Bible or learned at synagogue,' Derick said. 'History is written by the victors, and the Nazarene won. Conclusively. His version of events has been fed to you people for so long that you think it's the capital-T Truth. Heaven, Hell. Black, white. Good, evil. There's more to this universe than Manichean Dualism. There are more forces at play than The One. Or are you content to continue down the path you've been on all your life, which is essentially a dark alley between two fences guiding you to the slaughterhouse floor?'

They drove through an industrial part of town, crossing train tracks. Rumbling over them was the loudest sound inside this quiet miracle of Swedish automotive engineering.

'Do I really need to subscribe to your newsletter?' she asked. 'I'm here because you guys used to work with my mom.'

He turned a corner and suddenly they were in a neighbourhood carpeted with wall-to-wall, plush, manicured yards and large, Italianate McMansions.

'Let's be honest with each other,' Derick said, rolling up to a stop sign. 'You're here because we have guns.'

'That too,' she said.

He accelerated smoothly away from the corner, and at the end of the next street they entered a high-end commercial district with quaint brick sidewalks and very expensive boutiques.

'There's another thing you've learned about demons tonight,' he said.

'What's that?' she asked, suspicious.

'They really don't like your father.'

'We definitely have that in common,' she said.

A three-storey building made of tinted glass and peach marble with phony classical columns rose up before them. Derick drove past it, then made a hard left onto a ramp leading into a brightly lit, underground parking garage. They glided to the end of a row of gleaming luxury vehicles, and pulled smoothly into a space. Before taking off his seat belt, Derick gave her a look. He had piercing green eyes. She hadn't noticed before.

'You're not our prisoner, Ms Lieberman,' he said. 'You can leave at any time. However, our mutual dislike of your father means that we might find some common ground on which to develop a productive partnership.'

'Or I could cut my losses and go,' she said.

'But then you wouldn't know where your mother is,' he said.

'She's dead,' Amber made herself say. 'I have to learn to accept it.'

'Do you?' Derick asked. 'From what I understand, she should be with us shortly. So if you'd like to see your mother, and have your father face the consequences of his actions, well, your best option would be to follow me upstairs.'

CHAPTER 8

HE WASN'T RUNNING away, Father Glenn told himself. He'd made a strategic retreat. There was a difference. Amber would understand. Probably.

He ran through the woods, panting, throat raw, tripped over a waist-high wire fence, jumped a nasty ditch, then stepped in a puddle of what smelled like liquid shit. He was starting to realise why some cons got out of prison then turned right around and begged to be let back in. The outside world was a pain in the ass.

Amber would definitely understand, he told himself. They had mutual trust now, and according to her that was a two-way street. She'd learned that these supernatural shitheads were his area of expertise and he was the only one who could get her off their radar.

There had simply been too many guns in that construction site, and too many demons. The Asmodeus cultists had been a lot, but then to discover that the Atlanta PD was full of Satanists, well, that was more than one man could handle. Then those well-dressed yuppies had shown up and he'd heard them shouting and turned around just in time to see Belphegor himself squeeze out of a stretch limo – and if two cults of demon-worshippers were bad, three was downright intolerable. When had suburban Atlanta turned into a hotbed of demonic conflict?

He crossed a field and his right foot slipped in a dead possum and he went down. The poor marsupial had been there for a while and gotten pretty soupy. He wound up with it all over his pants. He wiped himself clean with handfuls of dried grass. He could be in Miami by now, but no, he had to try to be a good parent.

Belphegor, Ruler of the Gap, The Yawning Chasm, The Emptiness That Shall Not Be Filled. From what he could tell, Belphegor was running a law firm now, and it sounded like the same one Sheila'd worked for. That'd explain her disappearance. They'd probably hired Sheila for the same reason the Asmodeans kept an eye on Amber. They were all hoping he'd show up.

Father Glenn got most of the possum off himself and looked across the field to the highway. There was a Scotsman gas station down there and he could probably catch a ride with someone, get to the bus station, and get to Miami before sun-up.

Because really, what was he doing here? Atlanta contained three of the Seven Princes of Hell, and it looked like they'd all been waiting for him to show back up. They were pretty hacked off for what he'd done to them a long time ago, back when he'd been a much younger man, and he knew they could hold onto a grudge like Frank Sinatra. Smartest choice: blow out of town, head for Miami, and let them chase their own tails up here for a while. Eventually they'd realise he'd moved on, and they'd leave Atlanta alone.

Or he could hitch that ride back into town and find his daughter. As much as he hated to admit it, he was kind of responsible for this mess. Besides, if he didn't, well, this wasn't a strategic retreat anymore, was it? It actually was running away.

He really hated ethical dilemmas.

Derick led Amber to a conference room on the third floor and asked her to wait. She kept expecting to see something horrible around every corner, like she'd wandered into a dark carnival ride with a demonic theme, but it was all soothing earth tones and indirect lighting. Every time they turned a corner, her heart stopped, but so far it had been nothing but richly carpeted floors, inlaid wood walls, and tasteful regional art.

The conference room had an oil painting of dogs with ducks in their mouths at one end, and a pull-down screen at the other. The windows looked out on a dark parking lot, just starting to lighten with the dawn. There wasn't anything to read except a box of Kleenex. The carpet was the colour of honey, and every now and then the sound of human voices mumbling in other rooms lulled her to sleep. Her head snapped back and forth once, twice, then she gave up and burrowed her face into the crook of her arm and konked out.

The sound of the double doors opening snapped her awake. Her vision was grainy but she saw Derick coming in, carrying two white mugs. He put one in front of her and the smell of fresh coffee made her stomach growl. He sat beside her.

'Here's what we're thinking,' he said. 'We want a partner, not a prisoner.'

The coffee chased the fog from Amber's brain and the grain from her eyes. She nodded.

'Sure,' she said.

'We've been considering eventualities and we believe that your father is going to come looking for you,' Derick said.

'Yeah, right.' She gave an ugly laugh. 'He doesn't care about me, or anyone else. Even though I was the one who picked him up from prison.'

A light dawned in Derick's eyes.

'Ah,' he said. 'So that's where he was. We wondered why no one could find him.'

'How many of y'all are looking for him?' Amber asked. 'Or is that the royal "we"?'

'Seven, ultimately,' he said. 'We're not all on the friendliest terms but your father is a shared interest.'

'Well, I guarantee he's already on a bus headed out of town,' Amber said.

' I think you're underestimating yourself,' Derick said. 'You're of his blood. His only child. He won't be able to tolerate you being here with us. He'll come.'

'The only child we know of,' Amber said. 'He's probably got kids all over the place.'

Derick shook his head.

'Trust us,' Derick said. 'Lord Belphegor's resources are considerable. The only woman in whom he spilled his seed was your mother.'

'Okay, I don't need the details,' Amber said.

'Blood cries out to blood,' Derick said. 'He won't be able to resist some kind of misguided rescue attempt.'

Amber felt a twinge. After all, he was her father.

'Are you going to kill him?' she asked.

Derick gave a sad smile.

'The Great Belphegor's imagination is not so limited. We won't kill your father. Not for a long time. Not when there are so many other things to do with him.'

That didn't sound good to Amber; in fact, it sounded exactly like what a member of an evil Devil-worshipping cult would say.

'Where's my mom?' she asked, focusing on the important things.

'She'll be here any minute,' Derick said. 'The two of you will be free to leave, of course, but if you wait until your father gets here you'll both leave with our extensive gratitude.'

'Sure,' Amber said. 'Fine with me.'

Well, he *had* said that they weren't going to kill him. That was something.

'But first,' Derick said, 'there are a few changes we have to make.'

'To what?' Amber asked.

Derick flicked his eyes away.

'This and that,' he said. 'To you. Just a few alterations.'

He stood suddenly. Amber fortified herself with another sip of the impossibly good coffee, then followed him out of the conference room and down the hall. The building was filling up and a handful of good-looking, well-educated people dressed in soft greys and subdued beiges – and the occasional free spirit in seersucker — passed by, making brief but pleasant eye contact.

At the end of the hall, Derick opened a door that looked the same as every other door, except it opened into a room lined with bright white tiles – floor, ceiling, walls. There was a drain in the middle of the floor.

Amber suddenly had some doubts.

'What was all that about eating my womb?' she asked as Derick guided her to a padded black chair in the middle of the room.

'Lord Belphegor?' Derick asked, pushing her gently down into the chair. 'He can't resist a rhetorical flourish.'

She didn't feel so trusting all of a sudden.

The door opened and four women entered. They looked like they came from another dimension, so precisely groomed that they seemed stamped from a mould, not a hair out of place. They marched towards her, pushing two carts.

The tallest woman got her cart next to Amber, and opened the top to reveal a lot of glittering, sharp instruments.

'Wait,' Amber said, trying to sit up.

'Sssh,' Derick said. 'Don't fight it.'

'What are you doing?' Amber asked, panic clawing its way up her throat as the tallest creature picked up a sharp pair of scissors.

'You look a state,' Derick said. 'So we thought we'd give you a makeover.'

The tall woman dove in with her scissors and began to reshape Amber's bangs.

Father Glenn pushed his way through the door of Denny's. The scent of warm pancake batter and hot coffee immediately made him feel more human. Not many people were inside at six a.m., which was good because he looked, accurately, like he'd lost a fight with a wire fence and a dead possum.

He passed the 'Please wait to be seated' sign and zeroed in on a booth in the far corner, against the windows, under a large yellow-and-red decal offering a two-for-one biscuit deal tied in to the release of some new dinosaur monster movie Father Glenn hadn't heard of. A man sat in the booth.

The small, middle-aged Asian man turned the page of his *USA Today* then froze when Father Glenn reached his table. He looked up. Father Glenn looked down. The man wore black pants, a black shirt, and a priest's collar. He stared at Father Glenn through his reading glasses, his expression so closed it might as well have been a fist.

Father Glenn slid into the booth.

'Father Joe,' he smiled. 'How's it hanging?'

Father Joe watched him, stone-faced.

'That coffee sure looks good,' Father Glenn said. 'Smells like a fresh pot? You think I could get some?'

Father Joe didn't blink. Father Glenn looked around to see if the waitress was nearby, but she was talking to the fry cook on the other side of the pass, so he decided to get down to business. He hunkered forward, putting the most earnest expression he was capable of forming on his face.

'You remember that thing in Birmingham back about seventeen years ago?' he asked. 'Right around the time of the KISS *Rock and Roll Over* Tour?' Father Joe gave no indication of remembering any tour by KISS. 'You had that exorcism that kind of went sideways, and after I sort of quietly cleaned up your mess, you said, "Buddy, if you ever need anything, look me up." Well, it turns out that today I need something. And I wondered to myself, "Self, where would I find a man like Father Joe at this hour?" And my self said, "Remember how he said he was just a regular fellow? And regular fellows love Denny's. I bet you'd find him there, getting a full breakfast before beginning his pastoral duties." So I been walking around Atlanta looking in Denny's for the last two hours and, well, here I am, ready to take you up on your kind offer.'

Father Joe remained motionless. It was starting to feel kind of eerie.

'It's not a lot,' Father Glenn said, breaking the silence, trying to grease the conversational rails. 'All I need—'

Father Joe leaned forward slightly, but it felt seismic. Father Glenn stopped talking, stopped moving, stopped breathing.

'You dumb cunt,' Father Joe said. 'It was a fucking pleasantry.'

Father Glenn thought about that for a moment.

'A what?' he asked.

'Are you too fucking dumb to understand the word?' Father Joe hissed. 'Or do you need me to clean the shit out of your ears with my dick? Because I can stab you right through the ear with my motherfucking dick. Right this second, I can stick my dick through your ear canal, pierce your eardrum, and stab you in the fucking brain with it if that's what you want. Is that what you want?'

Father Glenn didn't know how to answer this cavalcade of phallic hostility.

'Well, motherfucker?' Father Joe asked. 'Is that what you want? My dick in your ear?'

'No?' Father Glenn tried.

'No, what?' Father Joe asked. 'No, what? You shit-for-brains.'

'No, I don't want you to stab me in the ear with your penis?' Father Glenn said, hoping this was some kind of code.

'Then get the fuck out of my Denny's, because that's what's going to happen if I have to look at your dumb fucking face for another fucking second.'

Father Glenn thought this had gone far enough.

'Now, look here,' he said. 'It's not "your" Denny's. It's—'

Father Joe cut him off.

'I like this Denny's,' he said. 'I am a frequent customer at this Denny's. When this Denny's had a problem with haunted condiments, I dragged the unclean spirit out and stuck its head up its own asshole and drop-kicked it back to Hell. So if I want to say this is "my" Denny's, then this is my motherfucking Denny's. Although now that you've dragged your saggy balls across its floor and polluted my favourite place with your rimjob breath, I'm going to have to leave "my" Denny's and never return. I may even have to burn "my" Denny's to the motherfucking ground. Why the *fuck* are you still sitting here?'

Father Glenn tried to figure how he could steer this conversation in a more productive direction. Father Joe stood up. He started to unzip his pants.

'Now hold on,' Father Glenn said, alarmed. 'There's no need for – aow!'

He screamed in pain as Father Joe picked up his cup of coffee and threw the hot liquid in his face.

'Christ—' Father Glenn began. 'AOW!'

This time, Father Joe bounced his now-empty coffee cup off Father Glenn's forehead. It hit the table, then rolled off. Quick as a snake, Father Joe grabbed it before it could shatter on the floor.

'Is everything okay, Father J?' the waitress, whose nametag identified her as Carol, asked.

'Might I have a refill, Carol?' Father Joe said, holding his cup out to her.

'Anything for you, Father,' she said, taking it.

He gave her a warm smile.

'Bless you, child.'

She smiled and went back to the wait station. Father Joe sat down again, staring hateful daggers at Father Glenn. The lower half of Father Glenn's face was scalded red and so was his neck. He rubbed an ugly dent in his forehead. His eyes brimmed with tears.

'Stop crying, you pathetic fuck,' Father Joe snarled.

'You hit me,' Father Glenn said, and his voice had a self-pitying hitch. Nothing good had happened to him since he got out of prison. He'd almost been murdered twice in the last twelve hours and getting scalded with hot coffee was more than he could bear. 'I've had a very long night.'

Father Joe rolled his eyes.

'You come in my favourite Denny's at five in the morning,' he said, 'crying like a bitch over some pleasantry I shat out of my mouth seventeen years ago. It makes me want to get unlimited refills so I can keep throwing them in your stupid face.'

'Here you go, Father,' Carol said, setting a mug of coffee down in front of Father Joe. Then she turned to Father Glenn, 'Did you want anything, sugar?'

'Is that a fresh pot—' he began, then saw an ugly look darken Father Joe's eyes. 'I'll stick with water.'

Carol left them alone. Father Joe picked up his coffee cup. Before he could throw it at him, Father Glenn said, 'I saw Belphegor.'

Father Joe stopped, hand frozen in mid-air.

'The fuck you say?'

'Not five hours ago,' Father Glenn said before anything else could get thrown at him. 'Coming out of a stretch limo, ugly as a haemorrhoid on a dinosaur's ass. He's got a whole cult going on down here, did you know that? A bunch of lawyers.'

Father Joe looked very sad.

'You piece of shit,' he exhaled.

'I know you've had a hard-on for him ever since New Orleans,' Father Glenn said. 'I've got business with him, too. He's here, in "your" town. He might even start fucking up "your" Denny's.'

Father Joe kept staring into his steaming mug of coffee. Father Glenn watched closely, looking for any indication that it was about to be thrown in his face. After a moment, Father Joe set it down and raised his furious eyes to Father Glenn.

'I'll tell you what you're going to do,' he said. 'You're going to write me a letter. And then, maybe I'll listen to your bitch-ass sob story, and maybe – *maybe* – after that I'll decide to see what I can do to help.'

'A letter?' Father Glenn asked, wondering if that was a code word for something terrible.

'Those dress-wearing sissies in the Vatican,' Father Joe snarled. 'They want us to embrace an ecumenical ministry. They've been chasing ten-year-old tail for so long they've forgotten that the true mission of the Church is to send Satan's minions screaming back to Hell. They think I don't do enough "inter-faith ministry". Your letter's going to testify to the opposite.'

He raised his coffee cup in a menacing fashion.

'I'll write you a letter,' Father Glenn said, quickly.

'You're damn straight you will, you pathetic fuck,' Father Joe said.

He took a quick, angry sip of coffee.

'Now,' he said. 'What the fuck is your problem? Why's Belphegor messing with your saggy old ass?'

'Well,' Father Glenn said. 'It's about my daughter.'

'You've got a daughter?' Father Joe asked.

For the first time, he looked interested.

'Yeah,' Father Glenn admitted.

'Where the fuck is she?' Father Joe asked.

'Well,' Father Glenn said. 'That's the tricky part.'

She didn't know how much time had passed and she didn't care. They'd washed her hair, done her nails, given her the bangs she never would have had the courage to try on her own. They'd rolled in a wardrobe rack and a man named Pie helped her pick pieces that went with her complexion (apparently she was a Sagittarian Autumn). She wore a suede skirt and a high-collared shantung top. They'd done her nails. She'd even been given a brief seated massage.

Everything that had happened to her last night felt very far away, as if it had happened to someone else. The door opened again, and this time Derick came in pushing yet another cart.

'Don't tell me you're a stylist, too?' Amber asked.

She felt luxurious, pampered, valued.

Derick smiled and parked his cart next to her.

'The finishing touch,' he said.

Derick settled her wrist on the arm of the chair. She let him. Something cinched around her wrist, and before she could react, he'd strapped her other wrist to the other arm of the chair with thick Velcro straps. He squatted and wrapped matching straps around her ankles before she could kick him.

'What're you doing?' she asked, struggling.

But the straps were too tight.

'You might want to close your eyes,' he said.

'Why?' Amber asked, remembering the drain in the floor. Was he going to kill her? In this building full of people who looked like they'd all been to Ivy League schools? Who were all in a cult! Oh, god, they were going to kill her. 'No!' she screamed.

'It won't hurt,' Derick said.

That did not sound very convincing coming from the man who'd just strapped her to a chair next to a floor drain.

'Fuck you,' she said, feeling like her father's daughter underneath these expensive clothes.

Derick sighed and pulled a black cloth off the thing on top of the rolling cart.

Amber strained her neck and saw a big, glass fishbowl. It looked empty – and then she saw something move. Something long and shiny and chitinous. Something with hundreds of scrabbling, hairlike legs. Something with pincers on both ends and no eyes.

Derick pulled it out with a pair of silver tongs. It was horrible and squirming, and thick as a garden hose.

'Oh, god,' Amber gasped. 'You're going to make me eat a centipede?'

The thing never stopped moving, twisting around itself, writhing.

'A millipede, technically,' Derick said. 'And actually, not even that. More of a Slurch.'

'...oh god... oh god... oh god...' Amber thrashed against the straps.

'And you don't have to eat it,' he said. 'It prefers the nose.'

It coiled around the end of the tongs, craning its blind face towards her. Derick brought it closer, so close she could smell it, and it smelled of dusty cockroaches and sun-warmed insect wings. She felt its hairy, squirming legs scrabble lightly against her lips and her gorge slammed into her sinuses.

She wanted to scream but couldn't open her mouth and so she made a loud *MMMM* sound. That's when it squirmed up her nose. It hauled its long, squirming body off the tongs and onto her upper lip then jammed itself up her left nostril, and she could feel its legs tickling the edges of her nostrils, she wanted to sneeze, but it filled her, filled her sinuses, its long bulk sliding up into her, up between her eyeballs. Then the tail end of the thing vanished into her skull and any chance of getting it out was gone.

'Oh god!' she screamed. 'I can feel it. I can feel it in my brain.'

The thought of this thing inside her skull felt filthy, dirty, she wanted to claw her face off and dig her fingers into her brain and drag it out, she felt like she'd never be clean again.

'Oh, please,' Derick said. 'There are no nerve endings inside your skull.'

Then he rolled his cart out of the room.

Amber cried, she sobbed, she tried to make herself vomit, she exhaled hard through her nose. She could feel it moving in her – *inside of her* – and she wanted it out. She felt its legs on the backs of her eyeballs, on her frontal lobe, its pincers digging into her soft, pink folds, her throat full of a putrid nasal drip that tasted of roasted insects.

She was contaminated. She was ruined. She was never going to be okay again.

Her head sagged to one side and she couldn't stop gagging, spitting up a thin green gruel down her new shantung blouse. It puddled in her suede lap.

The door opened, but she didn't bother to look up. Her queasy stomach just hitched and cramped as she spurted up another tablespoon of bile.

'Oh, sweetheart,' a familiar voice said. 'What did they do to you?'

Amber lifted her head and stared at her mother, standing in the doorway of the room.

CHAPTER 9

IT WAS DEFINITELY her mother. Wearing jeans and her favourite pair of red cowboy boots, a red blazer over a black top, her trademark Mickey Mouse watch on one wrist, shorter than everyone but always larger than life – it couldn't be anyone else. Standing in the doorway of this white-tiled Hell-room, the only person in the world who could make things better, the only person she could trust, the only person who loved her completely.

'Mo... mo... MOm...' she moaned through the curtain of mucous sheeting down her face.

'Sh, sh, sh, babydoll,' her Mother said, coming to her, wiping her nose with Kleenex. "That's a suede skirt.'

Her mom's desire to take care of her clothes made Amber's chest hitch as she bawled harder. She knew she needed to bring her up to speed, to tell her she'd tracked down her dad like she'd asked, and he'd shown up and ruined everything, and about the cultists or whatever they were, about shooting those three men in her apartment, about almost being murdered by the police, about coming here and thinking everyone was so nice until they put that (*monster, insect, thing*) up her nose. But she couldn't put the right words in the right order so all she could do was wail: 'Moooommmmm!!!!!'

Her mom disappeared behind her briefly to unstrap her ankles and wrists, and then she threw herself forward and her mother held her while she sobbed.

'There, there,' she said over and over again. 'It's all going to be okay, baby girl.'

She hadn't realised how much she missed her mother's small, strong arms around her, stroking the back of her hair, rocking her gently from side to side. She'd missed this so much. She just wanted to stay here forever, where it was safe. But, slowly and surely, she remembered where they were. She remembered how much danger they were in. She remembered the thing inside her skull.

'We have to go,' she said, standing on shaky legs. 'They're going to come back.'

'Who?' her mom asked.

'Where've you been?' Amber asked.

'That's complicated,' her mom said.

'Okay, first let's worry about getting somewhere safe,' Amber said. 'The people here are bad. Really bad. Really, really bad. They killed two people earlier tonight and they just tried to kill me.'

'They did?' her mom asked, stepping back, holding Amber at arm's length, looking her up and down. 'Because you look great.'

'Thanks,' Amber said, automatically. 'But—'

'When did you get bangs?' her mom asked.

'Just now. Listen—'

'That is a cute outfit, too.'

Amber felt like she needed to get this back on track.

'Mom,' she said. 'They put something up my nose...'

Even mentioning it made her lips quiver and hot tears start sliding down her face again.

'Sweetheart,' her mom said. 'I assume you've seen some things tonight that'll make what I'm about to say not sound totally off the deep end, but we're safe here. Gory has been a literal prince about letting me stay.'

'Gory?' Amber asked, confused.

'Belphegor, Ruler of the Gap, blah, blah, blah,' her mom said. 'He's a big deal in Hell. I know it sounds coo-coo but I'm guessing you're in a more receptive frame of mind than you were twenty-four hours ago. See, I got in trouble with some other one – Asmodeus, or something – and I panicked and didn't have anywhere to go, so Gory revealed himself to me and kind of gave me the rundown on the high-end, private client work we do at the firm, and the partners let me stay. They've got a really nice little guest suite. In fact, you could probably stay with me until everything blows over.'

'But, Mom?' Amber said. 'These are bad people.'

'Did they hurt you?' her mom asked, suddenly all serious concern.

'They gave me a makeover,' Amber said, and her voice got higher with hysteria. 'And they put a... they put something up my nose!'

She couldn't wrap her head around the horror that lived inside her skull, the fact that it was even there at all – wrapping its coils around her brain, filling the curved interior surfaces of her skull – made her feel sick.

'A Slurch,' her mom said, and shook her head. 'Those guys. Here.'

She took Amber by the wrist and pulled her out of the room behind her like she was five years old again. Amber felt the world return slightly to normal when her feet hit the rich red carpet in the hall. Her mom pushed open the expensive-looking wooden double door to the conference room and brought Amber inside. The air conditioning felt cooler in here.

'Have a seat,' her mom said, and started going through built-in cabinets at one end of the room. 'Do you want some water? Coffee?'

Amber pulled out one of the rolling chairs.

'No,' she said, carefully. 'I'm okay.'

She didn't know what else to do, so she sat down, keeping one eye on the door, expecting them to burst in with their guns and their fishbowls any second.

'Ah ha!' her mom said. 'I knew I'd find one. These guys love games.'

She sat down next to Amber and put a deck of playing cards in front of her.

'Deal me a hand,' she said.

'Of what?' Amber asked.

'I don't know,' her mom said. 'Poker.'

'I don't know how to play poker,' Amber said, wishing her mom would talk to her about things she understood again.

'Just deal,' her mom said.

Amber picked up the deck and her hands woke up at the ends of her wrists. For the first time in an hour, she forgot about the thing coiled inside her skull as she cascaded the cards one-handed, fanned them, did a riffle shuffle, bridged them, then performed a Butterfly Cut.

'Now do a classic force,' her mom said, and the Ace of Spades seemed to jump out of the deck. 'A Hofzinser Spread,' she said, and the Ace of Spades jumped out again. 'A Double Lift,' she said, and the cards screeched to a halt in Amber's hands and she flipped over the top card: the Ace of Spades.

Amber threw the deck on the table like it was made of snakes.

'What the Hell!' she asked, staring at them, chest heaving.

'It's the Slurch,' her mom said. 'They do this with people they trust. I keep telling them it's gross, but they can't help themselves. The Slurch teaches everyone a different little skill. It's like a disgusting housewarming gift. It means you're part of the family.'

'Do you have one?' Amber asked.

'Knitting,' her mom said. 'You should see my herringbone stitch.'

Amber looked down at the cards scattered on the table in front of her.

'I can play cards,' she breathed.

Downstairs, the revolving glass door spun lazily and spat Father Joe and Father Glenn into the black-and-white-tiled lobby of Volker & Leeman. All around them stood blond wooden walls displaying enormous spirals of grain. Overhead, the coffered ceiling was lit with tastefully recessed lighting. At the far end of the lobby stood a reception desk and behind it a swooping set of stairs leading to the second floor. Between the desk and the stairs an efficient young woman tapped on a PC.

They walked across the lobby and she looked up and smiled. She was trained not to let anything shake her poise, not even a priest and a scruffy looking hillbilly, arms purple with tattoos, coming in the front door before nine in the morning.

'Good morning, gentlemen,' she said. 'What can I do for you?'

Neither man said anything for a moment. They both stood awkwardly in front of her desk. The priest gave the redneck an annoyed look as if to prompt him. The redneck just looked around the lobby, taking in the obvious wealth, checking out the stairs to the second floor behind her. Finally, the priest gave her a tight smile.

'Good morning, my child,' he said. 'We're here to see Derick...'

At a loss for a last name, he turned back to the redneck.

'Derick what?' the priest prompted him.

'Abernathy,' the redneck mumbled.

'Derick Abernathy,' the priest smiled to her.

'Do you have an appointment?' she smiled back.

'I'm terribly sorry, my child, but no.'

'Well, I'm the one who's terribly sorry now,' she said. 'But Mr Abernathy is very busy. Maybe we can schedule something for later on with one of our other associates?'

She made her smile bigger. The priest flashed her a thin-lipped smile, then grabbed the hillbilly by the elbow and pulled him away from her desk. The two of them held a whispered conference in the middle of the lobby. At one point the redneck pointed at the ceiling. After a couple of minutes, the priest returned. She welcomed him with yet another smile.

'Did we decide—' she started.

The priest punched her in the face. She flew backwards out of her chair and hit the marble floor and lay limp. The priest didn't hesitate, he came around reception, walking quickly towards the stairs to the second floor.

'Let's roll,' he said.

Father Glenn scrambled to keep up.

❧

'So we can leave?' Amber asked.

She did classic table shuffles, in-hand riffles, and cascades. The faster her hands worked, the more the memory of what was living inside her skull faded.

'This is the safest place we can be,' her mom said. 'You're making me want to get my knitting needles.'

'It's crazy, right?' Amber asked.

Her hands kept flickering through the deck, turning over cards, palming them, exposing one after the other, then seamlessly sliding them back into the flow.

'I imagine all of this seems a bit crazy,' her mom said. 'You probably feel like you've gone through the looking glass.'

'If the looking glass was made of castrated lunatics trying to kill you,' Amber said, 'then yes, that's exactly how I feel.'

'Amber,' her mom said, leaning forward. 'I know things are overwhelming right now and it's hard to know who to trust, but believe me when I say that where we are is the safest place for both of us.'

Amber did a Faro shuffle followed by a Waterfall that ended in a quick fan.

'But can't we just leave and let them sort it out with Dad?' Amber asked. 'That's got nothing to do with us, right?'

She felt her mother go very still. With a great effort, Amber brought her hands to a stop and made herself look up. Her mom looked serious, lips pinched, eyes narrowed, breathing hard through her nose.

'You need to understand something, sweetheart,' she said. 'Your father has to die.'

Amber suddenly felt like she'd made a terrible mistake.

The three guys coming down the stairs looked like they might've played some high school football. One of them might have been a linebacker, but he was getting soft around the middle. The one in suspenders looked like a wide receiver with strong legs and a narrow chest. The third had to have been the quarterback. Even now, he glowed, the Golden God of some small Tennessee town, and in his eyes you could see all the girls he'd screwed in the back seat of his Mustang, all the mothers who'd looked at him with un-motherly eyes, all the fathers who'd breathed his name in the same tone of voice they reserved for the Lord God almighty.

They walked down the stairs, joking with each other about things only Atlanta lawyers would understand, mugs of coffee in their hands, not pausing as Father Joe strode towards them two steps at a time, Father Glenn scampering along in his wake. The wide receiver must have sensed something off because he stopped on the step directly above Father Joe, blocking his way.

'Excuse me?' he said.

A natural coward, Father Glenn froze, caught, his shoulders hunched up to his ears, but Father Joe simply stood there, head down, arms at his sides, studying the wide receiver's shoes.

'Can we help you with something?' the wide receiver asked.

Something moved through the air, too fast to follow, just a black blur smashing into his groin as Father Joe delivered a powerful right uppercut to his balls. The wide receiver dropped straight down but Father Joe was already stepping around him, spinning into an elbow hook that caught the quarterback in the side of his knee at 60 mph. As it buckled, he started to scream, but Father Joe was already slamming the heel of his hand into the quarterback's jaw, effectively cutting off both his scream and the tip of his tongue, and giving him a serious concussion.

Miraculously, the quarterback managed to hold onto his coffee, even as he keeled forward and slid to the bottom of the stairs on his face. The linebacker used this time to step away, putting his back against the banister. His hands went up in a classic boxing stance.

Father Joe ducked under his reach, grabbed him by the belt, and simply flipped him backwards over the banister.

'I'm sorry,' Father Glenn muttered as the linebacker's skull speared into the lobby floor with a wet crunch.

'With me,' Father Joe said, striding up the stairs.

'I only called him because you told me to,' Amber said, holding her hands still, realising the gravity of what she'd done.

Her hands itched. They craved the cards. She felt like she was in so much trouble. Her mom's face shifted seamlessly to empathy.

'It's okay, sweetie,' she said, patting her leg. 'You didn't do anything wrong. You only did what you thought was best. And it is best.'

She picked up the phone on the credenza by the door and punched three numbers for an internal extension.

'Derick,' she said. 'I'm in Conference Twelve, can you bring the Florida file? We need to fill Amber in on the bigger picture.'

She hung up and turned to Amber.

'I got messed up with a thing down in Florida,' she said. 'There was a whole timeshare lawsuit and I was trying to build a case and things just got out of hand and then, I know it sounds strange, but all these Satanic forces got involved. Gory was a port in a storm.'

'And he hates Dad?' Amber asked.

'All these different cults hate everybody,' her mom said. 'You know, sectarian violence, the IRA killing British people, the Serbs and the Croats in Yugoslavia, normal people like us couldn't possibly understand who did what to whom and why they hate each other so much, but it goes back centuries. They mostly only want to kill each other, so as long as we keep our heads down, we're not in any danger. Your father is a different story, though. He has to be dealt with or he's just going to make everything worse. For all of us. You'll see. It's going to be so much better when he's dead.'

CHAPTER 10

FATHER GLENN FOLLOWED Father Joe as he moved through the cubicles like a shark. An IT guy carrying a thick notebook computer stepped in front of him.

'Sir,' he said. 'Whose guest are—'

That was as far as he got. Father Joe spun 360 degrees and did something with the edge of his hand that was too fast for Father Glenn to follow. The IT guy staggered backwards, choking on splinters of thyroid cartilage suddenly clogging his throat.

'Oh, my god,' a lady lawyer said, standing up.

Father Joe ignored her, pressing forward, but then she had a desk drawer open and was pulling out a chunky black handgun, and maybe he had eyes in the back of his head because he ducked, snatched the notebook computer from the IT guy (now flat on his back, turning blue) and with a shuffling sidestep he slammed it into the side of the lady lawyer's head.

'So sorry,' Father Glenn muttered as he passed her limp body, sprawled over her desk.

'Stop cowering,' Father Joe snapped. 'We need to go up.'

As he strode down the central aisle towards the elevators at the far end of the floor, concerned associates and paralegals began popping their heads up over the partitions like prairie dogs. Father Glenn kept his head down, embarrassed. Also, he really did not want to get his face caught on a security camera.

'Sir, I think you ought to—'

Father Joe scooped up a ballpoint pen and jammed it into the young man's thigh. The man's leg buckled and he fell like an oak. Father Joe punched him in the ear as he went past, driving his head into the carpet so hard it bounced.

Father Glenn mouthed apologies to everyone he passed: the intern holding his broken nose, the young lady in the puddle of coffee with a fractured collarbone, the seersucker suited fellow curled up in foetal position, cradling his balls.

They reached the elevators and Father Joe pushed 'Up'. The door opened almost immediately: empty. They stepped inside and Father Glenn turned back to the office, one hand raised.

'I'm really very sorry, y'all,' he said.

Then the doors closed. They stood in the rising elevator like it was just another normal day in the office, and Father Glenn wondered if he should maybe try to ask Father Joe to do slightly less damage to people, then the elevator *DING*ed, and the doors slid open, and they faced what looked like a solid wall of security guards in matching, starched blue shirts.

'Fellas,' he said. 'I think there's been a misunderstanding.'

The doors started to close but one security guard blocked it with his thick forearm.

Father Joe grinned.

❧

'Amber,' her mom said. 'Your father is not a good person.'

'I know he ran out on us,' Amber said, ignoring the solitaire spread her hands laid out on the table. 'I know he kind of ruined your life. I know he's generally a grifter and a con artist.'

'You don't understand,' her mom said. 'He's bad in a cosmic sense. He's got everything the wrong way around and he's doing real damage to the world.'

'He sure damaged me,' Amber said, laying a nine of clubs on a ten of hearts. 'My DNA, I mean. I can't imagine how many broken chromosomes he passed down.'

'Honey, stop playing solitaire and look at me,' her mom said.

Amber made eye contact, but her hands kept moving.

'This isn't about you or me anymore,' she said. 'Your father is like a disease that's spreading. Did he tell you he killed almost two hundred people back in Kentucky?'

Amber hated her dad but she'd always assumed he was in prison for some kind of DUI or hit-and-run or something. The idea that he had a body count made her feel lightheaded.

'What?' she asked.

'Knock, knock,' Derick interrupted, coming through the door.

He put a cardboard banker's box on the table.

'Thanks, Derick,' her mom said, and began sorting through the box. 'Why don't you join us? It's time Amber learned the truth about her father.'

Derick pulled out a chair and sat.

'Didn't I tell you your mother was safe?' he asked, giving Amber a gentle smile.

Amber didn't smile back. She watched her mom riffling through files, stacking them on the table in sloppy piles. She felt impatient. She needed to know what this was all about.

'Your father believes he perceives the objective truth,' her mom said as she kept hunting through the box. 'He doesn't, Amber. What he sees are lies shaped by his pre-existing prejudices. That's why he's hurt a lot of people. That's why he's going to get a lot more people hurt. And that's why you're going to help us kill him.'

Amber's hands resumed laying out a game of solitaire.

Father Glenn poked his head around the elevator door. Father Joe stood in the carpeted hallway, surrounded by the security guards, mostly hourly workers from a local temp agency. None of them were moving. Blood dripped from Father Joe's fists.

'Let's go,' Father Joe said, and started down the red runner leading down a long hall.

Father Glenn crept off the elevator and followed him on tiptoes, trying not to be noticed. The first door Father Joe kicked open revealed a ring of lawyers sitting around a big table, a couple of pastry platters in the middle.

Not seeing Belphegor in the room, Father Joe turned to walk away, but these lawyers weren't having it. They charged. Father Joe snatched two pencils off a side table, and before the lawyers could rethink their life choices he was in the middle of them, stabbing thighs and ankles, driving sharpened points into groin muscles and kneecaps, using them to puncture lungs.

Father Glenn huddled outside the door, listening to the terrible sounds coming from inside. He really, really wished there was another way to go about this. After all, he was a lover, not a fighter.

❧

'Can't y'all send him back to prison?' Amber asked. 'I mean, he's committed a lot of crimes since he's been out. Something he's done has to have violated his parole.'

She laid a seven of hearts on a six of clubs.

'He served his full sentence,' Derick said. 'So he's actually not on parole.'

The files her mom dug through were started to interfere with Amber's solitaire. She didn't care, but her hands did. They laid a two of spades on top of some brochures that had spilled from one of them.

'This is a question of Universal Balance,' her mom said. 'He's broken something bigger than the laws of the United States of America. He's broken the world. There it is.'

She pulled out a very old file, worn ragged by improper storage. Amber wiped the completed solitaire game off the table and began to lay out another.

'Honey,' her mom said. 'I want you to see this, no matter how painful it is. A long time ago, your father spent time in a locked psychiatric facility. And he escaped. And a lot of people died in the process. These photos—'

An unobtrusive knock at the door interrupted and she froze like a VCR on pause. A redheaded security guard with a crewcut and a swollen, bloody nose poked his head in.

'Sorry, sir,' he said to Derick. 'May I have a word?'

Derick and the guard held a whispered conference while Amber's mom just sat there, not moving. Amber's hands started putting down cards and she couldn't help but notice the brightly printed, photo-heavy brochures that had spilled from one of the files. They were for a timeshare in Okahumpka, Florida. It must have been the case her mom was working on when things went wrong.

'Amber?' her mom said, and she looked up. 'I'll be back in a second. Don't move, okay?'

Amber felt panic rising in her chest as her mom, the one familiar face she'd seen in the past forty-eight hours of chaos, got up and walked to the door. Something crashed in the hall and a pair of hard thumps came from the other side of the wall. Her mom smiled reassuringly.

'It's just a little misunderstanding,' she said. 'I'll be right back.'

And she left Amber alone.

Father Joe kicked in a double door to reveal yet another conference room. Twelve Volker & Leeman junior partners sat around the table. Every single one of them turned their heads to the door and they all looked surprised. Except one.

'Oh,' Belphegor said from the other end of the table. 'It's you. I certainly thought I had enough security to handle a couple of cross-humpers.'

His body bulged over the sides of his chair, his multiple chins hung down to the middle of his chest, and something that oozed from his pores had stained the front of his dress shirt yellow. He looked red-eyed, exhausted, and run down. The entire room smelled like sulphur.

'Demon!' Father Joe barked, as he leapt onto the conference table and ran at Belphegor.

The enormous Prince of Hell squirmed, trying to get away, but he couldn't reach his two canes. Junior partners grabbed at Father Joe but he was too fast. He leapt, landing on Belphegor with both feet.

'Aurk!' Belphegor cried as his chair tipped backwards.

Junior partners swarmed Father Joe, piling on, kicking him, pummelling him. He punched one in the face and kicked out the teeth of another. He rose to the surface of the scrum of lawyers and called to Father Glenn.

'Help me!'

Father Glenn realised some of the junior partners had spotted him. He was going to have to get his knuckles dirty now. He didn't want to fight lawyers, but he figured he couldn't let Father Joe face this alone. He started towards the fray. Then he stopped.

He smelled something. A whiff of something familiar that he hadn't smelled in a very long time. He let his nose guide him to the door, teasing out a single strand of scent from the tight braid of smells: woman smells like shampoo, and moisturiser, and expensive moisturiser. Office smells like copy paper and erasable ink. Then, he caught it: a delicate touch of coconut, a bit of jasmine, a taste of bubblegum. It was coming from a half-open door at the end of the long hall. Bright white light spilled from it like the inside of a refrigerator, and it drew him on like a moth to a bug zapper.

'Don't you leave me!' Father Joe called, picking up a stapler as six lawyers tried to hold onto his arms.

Father Glenn drifted down the hall towards the door, his nostrils clinging to the delicate thread of this scent, leading him to the threshold and then inside. The room was covered in bright white tiles – floor, walls ceiling. A padded black chair sat in the centre, bolted to the floor, and in it sat his ex-wife.

'Hello, Glenn,' she said.

'Sheila,' he said, and it was the most relieved he'd ever felt.

His daughter had wanted him to find his ex-wife and here she was, and now all he had to do was find his daughter and he'd be done. He could wipe away a tear at their joyful reunion then get on a bus and be in Miami by sunrise tomorrow. The sense of satisfaction he felt filled him so wholly that it made all the throat-punching, nose-breaking, pencil-puncturing, and whatever it was Father Joe was doing to those poor junior associates with the stapler right now, seem worthwhile.

'Honey,' he said, walking towards her. 'I am glad to see you. Now I can tell Father Joe to stop hurting people.'

She stood up and he stopped, wanting to respect her personal space. He knew they hadn't parted on the best of terms, and while there were two sides to every story, he understood that she was probably not very interested in his.

'You had to screw this up, too,' Sheila said, but she wore a faint half-smile that made him think she was sort of teasing him.

'Yeah, well,' he said. 'Just the way I'm built.'

She stepped towards him, and he thought maybe she was going to try to kiss him, or at least come in for a hug. She'd been in a stressful situation, so maybe she wanted a taste of something (and someone) familiar. He rubbed his lips together to make sure they weren't too chapped. Nope, his lips felt soft as velvet. Lucky girl.

She stopped right in front of him, smack in the middle of his personal space, and he felt like he'd drunk a quart of brown liquor on an empty stomach.

'I can't believe you actually came,' she said. 'They told me this place was Glenn-proof. Some kinds of magical glyphs and wards.'

'Yeah,' he said, mouth dry. 'They probably buried a dozen unbaptised babies in the foundations, but I'm a lot harder to keep out than all that.'

'I wouldn't know about those sorts of things,' she said, airily. 'Demons were always more your scene.'

'Well, Amber's eager to see you,' Father Glenn said. 'And I'm eager to get out of town and away from this mess, so nobody better get in our way. Father Joe got a bad evaluation from his boss and he's in a foul mood. Why don't we make tracks?'

'You really think we're going to be a happy family again?' she asked, kind of nasty and sarcastic.

That's when Father Glenn noticed the drain in the middle of the floor. He'd never been in a room that had a drain in the middle of the floor for good reasons.

'Not up to me, and not really my thing,' Father Glenn said, trying to pick up the pace. 'But can you believe she came to me? When you went missing she ran right to Daddy, ain't that something?'

Sheila seemed to find that funny.

'Anyhoo,' Father Glenn said. 'Let's get this show on the road.'

It was probably too soon for kissing so he took her hands. They felt cold. Her expression didn't change. Father Glenn let go of her cold hands and cupped her cheeks.

They felt like raw chicken.

'Sweetheart,' he started. 'You don't feel...'

But he couldn't go on. She really, really felt like raw chicken. He smelled bologna and uncooked turkey.

'Oh no,' he said.

On the end of Sheila's neck, instead of his ex-wife's familiar face, he saw that he was cradling an uncooked Butterball turkey, gleaming pale yellow in the bright light.

'Oh, Sheila,' he said, and those two words contained all the disappointment in the world.

As he watched, she came into better focus. Her neck was made of deli ham, her fingers out of hotdogs, her feet inside those boots were probably skinless chicken breasts, and her toes were most likely Vienna sausages. This had never been his ex-wife. They'd built a Meat Mama to lure him in.

As he watched, she peeled away, one serving portion at a time, until the floor was covered in a pile of deli slices, canned ham, and sausage patties with the uncooked Butterball turkey resting on top. The whole room smelled like a deli counter no one had cleaned in weeks.

'Dad?' the voice came from behind him. 'Mom?'

He turned and saw his daughter standing in the doorway, face slack.

'What'd you do to your hair?' he asked.

She'd cut it so short she looked like a boy.

'Where's Mom?' Amber asked, and she raised her eyes to his and they were full of betrayal. 'What'd you do to her?'

He looked down at the pile of processed meat on the floor with a pair of red cowboy boots on top of it and then back at Amber. He realised what had happened.

'They tried to trick you,' he said.

'Mom was right here,' Amber said.

'No, she wasn't.'

Amber took a step backwards, stricken.

'I talked to her,' she said. 'She was alive. She came here to be safe and we were going to go home after this and everything was going to be okay.'

'Sweetheart,' Father Glenn patiently explained. 'That wasn't your mama. That was a pile of luncheon meats with a Butterball turkey for a head that was brought to life by ancient Sumerian magic. These cult people wanted to get your guard down for demonic reasons.'

'They were protecting Mom,' Amber said, shaking her head, not wanting to listen.

'No.' Father Glenn tried to explain. 'See these deli meats? That's your mama. Look, they even had it wearing her boots. I know how you must be feeling – ham and roast beef slices walking around in your mama's boots, pretending to be alive. That's an awful thing to see.'

The door swung wider and the yuppie from the construction site, the one in the douchebag suit, Derick Abernathy, stepped through.

'Is everything all right in here?' Derick asked, then he saw Father Glenn. 'Oh. It's you.'

Father Glenn took a step forward.

'How dare you disgusting monsters try to trick my daughter—' he started, but stopped when he saw Amber grab the man's hand in both of hers.

'He did something to Mom,' she said, panic rattling her voice. 'He made her disappear.'

'He knows some tricks,' Derick said in a calm voice, not taking his eyes off Father Glenn. 'He could have done worse than that to her. He might have killed the poor woman. He might have even sent her to Hell.'

Father Glenn sensed that he no longer had the upper hand. If he ever had.

'There's no shame in being tricked by a demon,' Father Glenn told Amber, trying to talk her down. 'That's what they do. They can trick everyone but Jesus. But even when my eyes are baffled, my fingers can still feel the Truth, and I can tell you that was never your mama no matter what it said or did.'

'Amber,' Derick said. 'Your father is a very dangerous man. Remember what your mother was saying? Two hundred people. Back in Kentucky.'

Father Glenn felt his guts go cold. She didn't need to know that. He opened his mouth, and for once in his life, nothing came out.

'He's an escaped mental patient, Amber,' the yuppie was saying. 'He doesn't want you to know the truth about him. He'll do anything to keep that from happening. Why else do you think he suddenly appeared when your mother was about to reveal his secrets?'

Amber's eyes locked on to Father Glenn's and he tried to put everything genuine he had into them.

'Is it true?' Amber asked.

'I—' Father Glenn began, but his brain wasn't working right. 'It's not like it sounds...'

Amber screamed. It echoed in the room, bouncing off the tiles, and Father Glenn covered his ears. It went on and on and it was full of betrayal. She thought she knew the truth about him, and it *was* the truth about him in a way, but it wasn't him. He needed to tell her, but that scream, it drilled into his belly button and made him feel sick to his stomach. When it finally stopped, Amber was gone. And so was the demon.

'Amber!' Father Glenn called and ran into the hall after her.

The yuppie was ducking into one of the conference rooms like a cowardly prick. He went after him.

'Asshole!' Father Joe shouted from down the hall. 'A hand!'

He stood in the middle of the hall, swinging an office chair to keep off a cluster of lawyers. He had one black eye and his clothes were torn. The lawyers didn't look much better. Father Glenn rattled the conference room doors: locked.

Father Joe hurled his office chair into the mob of lawyers, and stepped back to Father Glenn. They stood against the locked conference room doors, nowhere left to go.

'You better be prepared to go down like a man,' Father Joe said, and put up his fists.

Father Glenn didn't want to die in the hallway of some asshole law firm but he didn't think he had any choices left. They waited for the lawyers to rush them, but they didn't move. They looked around, confused. Something was going on at the other end of the hall. They looked that way, trying to figure out what was going on, and that's when the first grey-ponchoed maniac came screaming out of the fire stairs, hammer in his hand.

'Hail Asmodeus!' he shrieked, and fell on the nearest lawyer.

A mob of Asmodeus cultists spilled out behind him, and suddenly the hall was awash in violence again, only this time none of it was being directed at Father Joe or Father Glenn.

'What —' Father Joe began, then he saw Father Glenn grinning. 'What did you do?'

'Well, now,' Father Glenn said. 'I thought it might be a courtesy to let them know that their hated enemies were hogging all the fun. So I gave them a call at their favourite bar.'

The sound of sirens drifted in to them from outside; a storm of sirens, like half the Atlanta PD showing up.

'Did you know,' Father Glenn said, 'that most of the police in this town are Satanists?'

'You called them, too?' Father Joe asked, grudgingly enjoying the sight of Belphegor's lawyers having their ears gnawed off by Asmodeus' cultists.

'I figured everyone should be in on this.' Father Glenn smiled, then his grin fell. 'Oh, shit.'

Beneath his bruises, Father Joe went pale. At the other end of the hall, something huge and inhuman ducked through the fire door. It stood and revealed its awful form: the head of a bull on the body of a man. It stood seven feet tall, and the tips of its horns brushed the acoustic tiles.

The Great and Terrible Asmodeus was here.

It saw Father Glenn over the heads of the cultists, and bellowed an inhuman roar. Then it waded through the battling humans, charging at him. Father Glenn turned and rattled the locked conference room door. The demon got closer, bellowing again. Father Joe shoved him aside and kicked the doors open.

There was nothing inside the conference room, just tipped-over chairs, and the conference table, and in the middle of the conference table...

'Help me, you ass!' Father Joe said, jamming chairs under the doorknobs.

But Father Glenn stared at what was in the middle of the conference table: Derick, torn open from his chin to his groin, ribcage splintered and pulled wide apart. In the middle of his ruined, gaping torso, a flight of stairs ran down and down into darkness.

'Belphegor,' Father Glenn said. 'He took the Hell Stairs.'

'There're no other exits, you asshole,' Father Joe said, and Asmodeus roared, right outside the conference room doors. 'Where are we going to go, you stupid dick?'

Father Glenn looked around frantically. There were no other exits, no hiding places, no way out, except...

'Oh, Hell,' Father Glenn said, taking in the wall of windows. 'Not again.'

EPILOGUE

THE GREYHOUND TICKET agent stopped doing her word jumble and tried not to hate the frantic-looking young woman standing on the other side of the scratched plexiglass, tapping it with a quarter. She had her break coming in half an hour and she could finish her jumble then. She'd gotten too many write-ups lately and she didn't need to hear another lecture from her assistant manager.

'If you want a ticket, I need an ID,' she said, projecting her voice through the tiny hole in the plexiglass between them.

The woman dug in her purse and pulled out a driver's licence and thrust it through the window. Glynnis wondered why the hell was someone with a valid driver's licence was riding the dog, but it wasn't her job to ask questions. It was her job to make it to her break.

'I need a one-way ticket,' Amber said through the window. 'To Okahumpka, Florida.'

'It's a matter of trust!' Father Glenn said. 'No one trusts each other anymore, that's what's wrong with this world. Friend doesn't trust friend, husband can't trust wife, dog doesn't trust dog, and especially daughters don't trust their fathers and would rather cosy up with dark forces than believe that their daddy, who can explain everything, only has their best interests at heart.'

'Whatever, man,' the Bi-Lo cashier said. 'I still can't sell you beer before noon. State law.'

'That's what they said at Nuremberg,' Father Glenn shot back, storming out of the supermarket. 'It's later than you think, my friend.'

Outside, Father Joe leaned against a row of shopping carts, holding a bag of frozen peas to the knuckles of his right hand. In the distance, Father Glenn heard fire trucks converging on the offices of Volker & Leeman.

'I am finished with this business,' Father Glenn said to Father Joe as the two men walked across the parking lot. 'This whole father-knows-best, take care of the family, the children are the future teach them well and let them lead the way horseshit. I storm a demonic stronghold to rescue her from The Pit, I stare down two actual Princes of Hell before noon, and what does she do? Cozens with the enemy. I tell you, Joe, don't ever have kids because they will do nothing but break your heart.'

'I have six,' Father Joe said.

Father Glenn stopped walking. They'd reached the sidewalk and mid-morning traffic flashed by.

'*Six!*' he exclaimed. 'You're made of tougher stuff than me. No, sir, I am done with this nonsense, that girl is out of my hair and good riddance. I tried, no one can say I didn't give it my best effort, but I swear, Joe, if I ever get the fatherly urge again you have my permission to beat me senseless with a two-by-four.'

Father Joe thought about this for a minute, then stepped forward and punched Father Glenn in the stomach. He doubled over, coughing.

'Stay out of my sight,' Father Joe said. 'Get out of my city. If I ever catch you in Atlanta again, I'm going to rip out your spine and beat you to death with it. Go with God.'

He threw the thawing bag of frozen peas at Father Glenn. It bounced off his head and hit the sidewalk, then he stalked away. Father Glenn braced his hands on his knees, and after a minute he was able to breathe normally again and pushed himself upright.

'And screw you, too, buddy,' he called to Father Joe's distant back.

He looked around the bleak Atlanta crapscape.

'I wouldn't stay in this literal Hellhole if a Dallas cheerleader got down on her knees and begged. Three demonic cults fighting over turf and all of them with a hard-on for this servant of God? No, sir. I seek greener pastures. Biggest disappointment of my life, getting out of prison and seeing how far this world has fallen. If God's got a plan, it is a poorly considered one. I want no part in it.'

He stuck out his thumb and was surprised when a 1981 Chevy Malibu instantly pulled to a stop and a middle-aged fellow in a Hawaiian shirt leaned across the front seat.

'Need a ride?'

'Sure do,' Father Glenn said. 'I'm headed to Miami.'

'I'm not going that far,' the man said and unlocked the passenger door. 'But I can get you almost all the way.'

Father Glenn slid in.

'How far are you going?' he asked.

'Okahumpka,' the man said, pulling out and dialling in some Hawaiian-ish music on the radio. 'From there you can get just about anywhere.'

'Sounds good to me,' Father Glenn said. 'And good riddance to all this.'

He waved his hand airily behind him as the Chevy Malibu bore him south, towards a small bedroom community just outside Orlando, a place known for its plenitude of lawsuits and timeshare condos.

Don't miss the next exciting instalment in America's number one supernatural action series:

THE REDNEXORCIST

_____**The Rednexorcist #2: Occult Orgy in Okahumpka!** **£3.49**
Florida burns with horny Hellfire as Father Glenn finds Amber in the one place no father should ever have to find his daughter: a haunted swingers' club! Black magic is the ultimate aphrodisiac in this sleazy sinpit, where the only exit leads straight to Hell!

_____**The Rednexorcist #3: Havana Hellhole!** **£3.49**
A red-blooded American like Father Glenn never thought he'd wind up in a Communist hole like Cuba, but the people of Castro's failed nanny state need the power of the Rednexorcist or they'll meet a fate worse than eternal damnation at the hands of literal Godless Commies!

_____**The Rednexorcist #4: Arkansas Bloodbath!** **£3.49**
Father Glenn returns to his roots and confronts his past when five of the seven Princes of Hell rise up in Little Rock! It's enough to make the Statue of Liberty weep when one of them declares it's a candidate for the President of these United States!

_____**The Rednexorcist #5: North Dakota Necromancer!** **£3.49**
A demonic narco-terrorist appears in the American heartland bent on a mission of supernatural destruction, and Father Glenn must destroy this wizardly pimp with his bare hands, only to discover that it's taken on the guise of famed country-and-western singer, Willie Nelson!

The Eden Book Society

DEAD INK BOOKS
375b Smithdown Road, Liverpool, L15 3JJ

Please send me the books I have checked above. I am enclosing a cheque/postal order (delete as appropriate) for £_______ (please add 35p per copy to cover postage and packing).

Name: ____________________ Address: ____________________

____

The Eden Book Society is made possible by the kind support of its patrons. In 1993, those patrons were...

Ad Edgley
Adam Farquharson
Adgee Harville
Adrian Baker
Adrianne Driver
Aisling
Aksel Dadswell
Alec Fullerton
Aletin
Alex
Alex
Alex Mills
Alexandria Trujillo
Alison Fields
Alison Moore
Aliya Whiteley
Amanda Dorsey
Amanda Irle
Amanda Nixon
Amelia
Anabel Escareno Green
Anastasia Martynova
Andi Wilson
Andrea Blackstock
Andrew Broussard
Andrew Crowl
Andrew Franklin
Andrew Fry
Andrew Hutcheson
Andrew Kozma
Andrew Leon Hudson
Andrew Stoehr
Ann Smith
Anna Mack
Anthony Higgins
Anton
Aristotelis
Art
ArtistSomeday
Ash Draighean
Ashley
Ashley Reedy
asuberu
Austin Alderman
Bandcloud
Bart De Sutter
Ben
Ben Brock
Ben Nichols
Benjamin Achrén
Benjamin Judge
Benjamin Poole
Beth
Blair Rose
Borja Bilbao
Bradley Adams
Bradley Walker
Brian
Brian Price
Carl Taylor
Caroline Coriell
Caroline Evans
Carolyn Stephenson
Cat
Catherine Miller
Catherine Spooner
Charlotte Geater
Charlotte Goulder
Chris
Chris Chambers
Chris Huning
Chris Johnstone
Chris Phillips
Chris Waldock
Christian Roulleau
Christopher Clark
Christopher Gritt
Ciaran sundstrem
Claire Fuller
Clare Dean
Clare Logan
Colleen Gordon
Connor Campbell
Connor Girvan
Conor
Conor Griffin
Contrary Reader
Courtney Button
Craig Hallam
Cristobal Eblen
D Franklin
D Mayo-Wells
Daisy Arendell
Damien Ryan
Dan Coxon
Dan Howarth
Dan McCormick
Dani
Daniel F.
Daniel Jolley
Daniel Lapinski
Daniel Molitiak
Danielle Nelson
Daphne Hoover
Daria Yocco
Darren Jackson
David Clayton-Wagner
David Hartung
David Thirteen
Dawn Driskill
Dean McLeod

Debbie
Denver
Diana Tanaka
Dipika Mummery
Dorothe Santistevan
Dragon's Roost Press
E. Beverly
Edward Abbott
Eileen
Eilíse B
Elaine Hernandez
Elle Hinds
Ellie
EMcD
Emily Kardamis
Emily Ormondroyd
Emily S.
Emma Striegel
Emma Watts
Eric Ania Haley-Halinski
Erica Fioritto
Erich the Wizard
Erika Steiskal
Erin Congdon
Esme Weijun Wang
Ethan Kaye
Evelyn
Evie Vincent
Ferus Dóttirson
fi3rwr
Fiona Donson
Fiona Findlay
Flora Tonking
Francesca
Francesca Killoran
Frankie
Gabrielle Hahn
Gavin Hower
Gavin Pugh
George Jack
George Sandison
George Stankow
Georgia Letten
gesina
Gillian Best
Gillian Thomas
Gina Boiardi
Gina Collia
Giusy Rippa
Glen Davies
Goats Flying Press
Grace Wallace
Graham Bailey
Gregory Monk
Guillermo
H Beasley
Hannah
Hannah Green
Hannah Levinson
Hannah Stein
Harlequide
Haunted Doug
Hayley
Hazel Turner
heather
Heather Klebs
Hel
Herdis Jakobsen
Hette
Hollie
Holly Kybett Smith
Hunter Sims
I Shibes
Ian Chung
Ian Critchley
Ian Mellett
Ian Mond
Imogen Eddleston
Imogen Robertson
Isaiah Scandrette
Jack Connell
Jacob
Jade
James
James Burrell
James Pickard
James Salwen
James Shaw
Jamie Lee Pilkington
Jason Scott
Jeanine Long
Jef Feyaerts
Jeffrey Coleman
Jeffry Pretes
Jen
Jen Smith-Furmage
Jenna
Jennie Moran
Jennifer Hackett
Jennifer Harper
Jennifer Homer
Jenny
Jeremy Steel
Jess M
Jess Popplewell
Joelle
Joey Peacott
John Barfoot
John Chapman
John Hedley
John J Sears
John Newman
John Wirkner
Jon Shaw
Jonathan Harker
Jonathan Laidlow
Jonathan Thornton
Joseph Camilleri
Joshua Cooper
Joshua Simmet
Judith Mckenna
Julia Cluney
Julian Koslow

Julian Simpson
Julie G
Juliette Guido
Justin Bright
Justin Passino
Justine
Kaleb Grant Lantrip
kangeiko
Karen Wenborn
Kat
Kathleen Towers
Kelly Hoolihan
Kerry
Kevin Sheets
Kieran Quinn
Kiran
Kirsty Syder
Kristina
Kyle
Kyle Druding
Laura
Laura Argenziano
Laura Elliott
Laura Miatt
Laura Probett
Lauren Morris
Laurent Weber
Lazarus Press
Lee
Leigh Barry
Lena Valencia
Levi
Lewis Birchon
Lindsey
Lise Mendel
Liz Hamilton
Lizzy
Lloyd Stephen
Lori Miller
Lorna
Louise Titheradge
Lucy R Hinnie
Lukas
Mac Marshall
Macarena Cabrera
Madeleine Pearce
Magdalena Birkmann
Manon
Mao
Marc Chernoff
Margaret
Maria Pilar San Roman
Marie-Anne McQuay
Mark
Mark James
Mark O'Neill
Mark Roseberry
Mark Wandra
Martyn Walker
Matilda Williamson
Matt
Matt Houck
Matthew Cavanagh
Matthew Craig
Matthew Hudson
Matthew Schwemlein
Maxim Jakubowski
Maxine Peake
Meg Sophie
Megan Boing
Melek Kilic
Melissa Henry
Melody Ellis
Michael
Michael
Michael Paley
Michelle Souliere
Michelle Stubbs
Mike
Miłosz Mazur
Miro Drury
Missy Mazzaferro
Mr. Push
MW
Myles Bush
Naomi 'nyoom' Watson
Naomi Booth
Naomi Morauf
Natalie Marshall
Nathan Ballingrud
Nathan Beal
Nathan La Porte
Ned Raggett
Neil Salvesen
Nellie Jackson
Niamh Kelly
Nick Badagliacca
Nick LaRocque
Nick Morandi
Nick Wilson
Nicky
Nicola Haden
Nicole Carrano
Niels
Nikki Brice
notasfarwest
oblongpictures
Olivia de sausmarez
Olivia Wolfenden
Ollie Langmead
P. Russ
Pandora Nethsingha
Pat Ashe
Patricia Blanchard
Paul Howard
Paul Vincent
Paul Walker
penguinonstrike
Peter Farr
Peter Schueler
Pharmcat
Philip Lynch
Philippa S

Pierre Demery
Piper Huxley
Pippa W
Priscilla Aguilera
Rachael Smith
Rachel
Rachel Darling
Rae Leaver Rahman
Ramona Howard
Rants
Raven Steele
Ray R.
Rebecca
Rebecca Hassall
Rebecca Kirk
Rebecca Lea
Rebecca ONeill
Rebecca Tonks
Rebekah Babb
Rebys Hynes
Red Newsom
Reece James
Reggie Chamberlain-King
Reina Cruz
Renee
Rhiannon
Rhodri Viney
Richard Grainger
Richard Martin
Ro MacCabe
Rob Bockman
Rob D
Robert Espy
Rose Walls
Rosie Morgan
Ruby Howe-Shepherd
Ruth Ann Orlansky
Ryan
Ryan Fisher
Ryan Todd
Sabine MacMahon
Sally A. Johnson
Sam
Sam Ainsworth
Sam Burton
Samantha Anderson
Samantha Fisher
Samuel Gardner
Samuel Skold
Sara
Sarah
Sarah
Sarah
Sarah Arkle
Sarah Avampato
Sarah Baker
Sarah Bodman
Sarah Kocich
Sarah Mae Goebler
Sarah Moreman
Sash Taheri
Seth Lee
Sheena
Sidney Leedham
Siobhan Dunlop
Skye Sisk
Skylar
slamdunkrai
smilesallday2
Sophie
Sophie Chappell
Soren Pears
Stefan Anderson
Stefanie Caeners
Stephanie
Stephanie
Stephanie Hilton
Steve Birt
Steven Holness
Steven Roman
Stevie
Stewie
Storymix Books
Susan Bohan
Tabitha Geist
Tami Lynn Giordano
Tass Pett
That Long Boy
theunlikelyone
Thomas Newton
Tiernan Blanchard
Timmy
Timothy Jarvis
Tobias Carroll
Tobias Paul
Tobias Selwood
Toby Jennings
Tom Clarke
Tom Isham
Tom Jordan
Tom O'Dell
tomtomgoose
Tor
Tracey
Tracey Thompson
Verity Holloway
Vince Haig
wasuremono
Weronika Mamuna
Wil
Wild Hunt Books
Will Smith
willbutler
William Gallimore-Tallen
Y Y Zhed
Yemeth
Zachary Locklin
zax724
zilla901
Zosha

The Eden Book Society is an open literary hoax that encourages readers to suspend their disbelief. It is a project put together by Cinder House Publishing Limited.

Cinder House Publishing is one of Arts Council England's National Portfolio Organisations. If you would like to keep up to date with what we're up to, check out our website and join our mailing list.

www.deadinkbooks.com | @deadinkbooks